blue girl,
yella fella

Lothian YA Fiction

Blue Girl, Yella Fella, Bernie Monagle

Dear Venny, Dear Saffron, Gary Crew & Libby Hathorn

The Devil's Own, Deborah Lisson

Dreamcatcher, Jen McVeity

Edward Britton, Gary Crew & Philip Neilsen

Fat Boy Saves World, Ian Bone

Golden Prince, Ken Catran

Mama's Babies, Gary Crew

Murder in Aisle 9, Jim Schembri

Red Hugh, Deborah Lisson

Ridge, Dorothy Simmons

Settling Storms, Charlotte Calder

Snigger James on Grey, Mark Svendsen

So Much to Tell You, John Marsden

Stalker, Hazel Edwards

Talking to Blue, Ken Catran

Tin Soldiers, Ian Bone

Video Zone, Dorothy Simmons

Voyage with Jason, Ken Catran

Welcome to Minute Sixteen, Jim Schembri

blue girl, yella fella

bernie monagle

Lothian
BOOKS

For my strong, smart and beautiful daughters,
Phoebe and Hannah,
and for Marisa. Have I told you lately?

ACKNOWLEDGEMENT

My thanks go to the students and staff of Sacred Heart College,
Kyneton, for both their technical assistance and moral support.
My thanks especially to all those who shared the story.

Visit the author's website: www.berniemonagle.com

Thomas C. Lothian Pty Ltd
11 Munro Street, Port Melbourne, Victoria 3207

Copyright © Bernie Monagle 2000
First published 2000
Reprinted 2000

National Library of Australia
Cataloguing-in-Publication data:

Monagle, Bernie.
Blue girl, yella fella
ISBN 0 7344 0091 8.
I. Title
A823.4

Cover design by Michelle Mackintosh
Cover photographs by Sonya Pletes
Text design by Paulene Meyer
Printed in Australia by Griffin Press Pty Limited

epic
beginnings

'The only rule is that you don't kill off the story.' Mungrel was feeding sticks onto the fire as he spoke.

It was hard to concentrate on what he was saying; Dicko was trying to cook our sausages. He was trying to pour more methylated spirits into the camp cooker before it went out. I backed off. I thought he and the fuel bottle were about to explode. He just managed to splash flaming metho on himself and his sausages, igniting the fat and doing a fair impersonation of the towering inferno. Dicko was dancing around trying to put himself out; it's a good thing metho burns cool. Mungrel slid a billy lid onto the sausages, putting them out.

'I said not to put the fuel bottles anywhere near a naked flame.' He was looking at Dicko, extinguished now but still smoking. 'Were you listening?' Dicko smiled that goofy look he gets. He was waving his hands at the smoke in the hope it would disappear. Mungrel muttered, 'Silly question', picked up the fuel bottle and put the lid on.

Dicko looked like he was having fun. 'The sausages look done,' he announced proudly.

'They look like burnt dog's turds,' observed Adam sourly as he gingerly lifted the smoking lid; he was sharing the cooking with Dicko.

'This epic you were talking about, where you're not allowed to kill off the story, is it like shared story in Theatre Sports?' asked Anna. Anna always understood, always asked the right question. I didn't know what the hell he'd been talking about. Mungrel hadn't ever taught me; I'd only arrived the year before last. He'd taught everyone else in year seven drama and some in history. They were pleased we'd got him for camp.

Adam was trying to eat the sausages wrapped in bread, dripping with sauce. 'These taste like . . .'

'Metho!' supplied Mungrel. 'So will every-thing you try to cook in that pan for a while.'

'I'm not eating this!'

'Thanks very much.' Dicko grabbed Adam's sausage in bread and crammed it into his mouth.

'You're disgusting!' Anna announced.

'Fank you!' exploded Dicko spraying crumbs, sausage and sauce.

Anna was brushing herself down but turning her attention to Mungrel again. 'This epic, we still share it?'

'Yeah, we share the story, but it can be much grander than a simple story. That's why I call it the epic. It can take the whole week of the walk if you like. 'What we do . . .' Mungrel began, as Kelly and Becc raced up from the river and fought over a piece of log. The dark shadow of the gorge wall was chasing the rest of the kids over to the fire; they had finished burning their dinner. Mungrel waited until he had their attention. He seemed pleased that the fire and the night were drawing the group together.

'What we do,' he began again, 'if you want to, is share an epic. We make it up as we go along. One person makes up a scene—you can tell it like a story or a film, invent works of art, poems, pieces of music, use whatever images or ideas you like. Then we all think about it as we walk along. We play with the ideas until someone else comes up with the next scene, then we share that. The only rule is that you don't kill off the story.'

I didn't think anyone would be in the mood for drama games. The day had been really hot. Marjorie had flaked out before lunch-time— apparently she always did that, she just flaked. I remember the teachers saying it's anxiety as well as heat, but I reckoned it was just attention-seeking. Mungrel called it an attack of the vapours; I don't know what that means exactly but I reckon he thought it was attention-seeking, too. Funniest thing is that when she faints there is always a teacher handy and she never hurts her-self, she just sorta slides to the ground. Me and the guys had been doing this new dance we'd invented, we called it the slide. We'd stagger around, wave our arms about until we'd do this graceful slide onto the ground. No one thought it was funny except us. But I think the girls were a bit pissed off with Marj.

We'd walked ten Ks that first day. It was sup-posed to be the easiest day because it was flat and just along the river but I was stuffed and I knew the girls were too; we'd been talking while we were swimming before tea. It was the packs. Normally my Docs are really comfortable but the weight pushes your feet into the front of the boot and I had blisters on both little toes. Tanja had a ripper on her heel.

I'd thought the camp was going to be great because, with Brad not coming, there were only four guys in our group. It was me and Matt, plus Dicko and Adam. Just the four of us and ten women! Unfortunately, there were also three staff. If you knew Adam and Dicko you'd know there wasn't much competition, just Matt. Even though Matt looks like that red-haired kid from the Rugrats cartoon the girls seem to like him. He's good at art and for some reason he's always talking to girls; I'm not sure who's cracking onto who.

Marjorie's flaking did us all a favour though; we got to swim every time we stopped, all the way along the river; we were really taking our time. The teachers were right about one thing—there were some great swimming spots and there was a lot more water in the river than the teachers expected. Before the serious autumn rains the river is usually pretty low although in winter it always floods. They say it is really a series of water holes in summer but a torrent in winter. The swimming made for some great booby watching. Funny though, Kelly who's got the best bod kept her T-shirt on and the others, who ain't bad, but not diamond-cutter good, let it all hang out. Maybe just as well. Adam and Dicko couldn't cope with that kind of exposure. I hoped we'd get a look by the end of the camp. No offence, Kell. It was supposed to be cooler the next day, so I didn't like our chances.

Miss Tish seemed cool; she was the only female teacher but she's not very old. She seemed really laid back, talking music; she's really into modern stuff, not techno but alternative stuff. She wasn't saying much at the campfire. The fire was really throwing sparks because the wind had come up. It was the start of the cool change; the sound of the wind ripping through the treetops was great; the temperature was dropping out.

Then this rainsquall hit, just a few drops really. By the time we got the tent flaps tied, it had passed and everyone trooped back to the fire. I reckon Mungrel had spooked us that morning. As we left the bus and rounded the first bend in the river he had stopped and told us that the State Emergency Service hated this gorge because every year they had to search for lost hikers.

He said that every few years someone dies out here—talk about instil confidence in us. Then he did this dramatic thing. His eyes went queer and he said, 'If you don't treat the bush with respect, it can kill you.' Then he went on about not getting off the track, not leaving the camp unless we told the teacher where we were going, all that sort of shit. He told us the whistle and cord he had issued us with was for emergencies only, he didn't want to hear them unless it was a real emergency and that we should wear them all the time.

Must admit as the sun went down I was glad about the fire, and I didn't fancy going any further from the fire than the tent. Although that was dangerous enough once Adam started farting. As I watched it get darker it seemed the shadows were creeping out of the bush and creeping as close to the fire as they dared.

It was right though, what Mungrel said. I walked up the hill to have a leak, turned around twice and everything looked the same. Freaky really, because it looked all safe and pretty like a painting, especially once you got away from civilisation and the blackberries. But I got a real shock. I thought, shit I'm lost! How could I get lost so easy? The bush looked all the same—I had no idea where the camp was or the river. My heart was pounding. I could hear it in my ears. I broke out in a sweat. I can't remember ever being so scared. Then I realised I could hear the rest of the class yahooing down by the river.

When I got back to the group Mungrel was watching me come out of the bush. 'Next time let us know where you're going, okay?'

I nodded. I felt that he knew I'd had a fright, he'd noticed me go into the bush and he'd been keeping an eye on me.

It was a great spot. We couldn't see the stars because of the clouds, but the wood smoke, the sound of the river and the wind was wild. Best of all, all the dickheads were in the other groups.

Nancy turned up at the fire in clean jeans with her hair brushed—I don't believe how stuck up she seemed. She'd spent fifteen minutes finding a non-slimy bit of the river to get out of. I'm amazed she got into the river in the first place. I guess it was as close to a shower as any of us was going to get for the rest of the week. Some of the girls went berko when they found out, said they weren't going.

Miss Tish said you all end up smelling the same so that no one can smell anyone else; she also had a chat with the girls about periods and stuff. We might smell the same until we get on the school buses to go home, suffer! No one could smell as bad as Adam, but no one.

Poor old Brad hadn't made it. Someone must have dobbed and they went through our packs. Brad is a real piss ant, he had this half bottle of sherry in a coke bottle; he really needs the stuff. He was going crazy with the idea of a week without a drink. It's not like he had a slab for a wild booze party.

At least he told them we didn't have anything to do with it. He spent the whole week at home having a holiday and probably drinking himself silly—that is if his old man didn't beat the shit out of him for getting caught with booze. I don't know what my old man would do; I was just glad I wasn't going to find out.

By the time it was really dark the girls had got into what soaps they were watching on telly, who was sleeping with who, who was double timing who, who had come back from the dead. The guys then got onto babes, then the girls hung shit on the guys for being sexist, and then bitched about the soap girls for having silicon boobs—except Kelly; she didn't need to be jealous of anybody. All of a sudden there was this bloodcurdling howl. It scared us shitless and then went echoing down the valley.

The fire cracked and collapsed and everyone jumped again, someone started to giggle and everyone spoke at once. It was Dicko, he's such a spaz. He was in his tent pissing himself. He'd really sucked us in, that howl freaked us out. Then we slagged him off so bad, like people do when you scare the shit out of them. At least we couldn't swear too much with three teachers there. You really only notice how foul we are to each other when there's adults around. We really hang it on each other and call each other disgusting things. I reckon our olds would faint if they heard.

Anna was still telling Dicko how immature he was—like, since when did he have to be told, again!—when Matt starts asking Mungrel about this epic.

'It's just what people used to do, before TV,' Mungrel said. 'Someone would tell a story and someone else would add a bit because they had a different version. Someone who heard it second-hand might add a bit to help their family understand why it was funny or whatever. And so on, until everyone heard the story. The really good stories would be told so many times they would be almost unrecognisable; they would sometimes get handed down for years. The next step I guess is people start inventing stories. I guess video clips are the closest thing these days, really creative storytelling. With this epic I like to think I'm a film director; I have this huge budget so I can make anything happen, so there aren't any limits. I can tell any number of stories at once, I can be really indulgent, it doesn't matter if some bits don't make sense.'

Matt was scratching the six red hairs on his chin he calls his beard. 'But you said you can share the epic?'

'Yeah, taking turns with a bit of time in between to think up the next part.'

'But how do you make the bits fit together?' Matt asked.

'Well, let's say I start the story, I tell the first chapter. Then you think about where I end it and decide where you want the story to go next.'

'Do one now?' Matt asked.

'The epic takes a while; it takes longer when you share the ideas,' Mungrel warned.

'Just a quick one,' Matt was keen. He's into that sort of stuff.

'Okay, Matt. I'll start and you see where you can take it. Just a quick one to practise. Let me think.' Mungrel put his head down and the silver in his crewcut shone in the orange glow from the coals.

'Wait for me,' shouted Tanja and then half the group fled to their tents returning with jumpers and sleeping bags. It was going to be one cold night. Those who didn't head for their tents moved the logs around and stole people's seats.

'Okay... The epic begins,' breathed Mungrel. He closed his eyes and lowered his head as if he were about to drift off to sleep. He was just thinking.

I've seen Mungrel, or Mr Mundle, he calls himself Mr Mungrel, walking down the corridor at school, all by himself, laughing himself sick. He's either a little crazy or enjoying himself a lot more than anyone else I know at school is. He looked up all of a sudden and stared around until he had everyone's attention. Then he began.

Mungrel's bit

It's dark. There is a glow. It fades. Again the glow. We realise we are seeing through the eyes of someone smoking a joint. It glows again...

'Alrriight!' cheered Adam, but he was hissed into silence.

It glows again, followed by coughing. There are voices murmuring, we can't really hear what is being said. The coughing starts again as we lurch through a door into the glare, blinding us with harsh kitchen light. We get deafened by some frantic thrash music. We see a collage of heavy partying. We get offered more booze. We are already swaying. We swig some neat vodka.

A persuasive male voice says to sit on his knee; someone asks if we are all right. We endure the sickening journey to the toilet. Someone is already there. We lean against the door and then stagger out the front door and onto the lawn. There is a sound of vomiting as our view falls onto the grass and blackness. The sound of the party music recedes as our vision clears to show us a yellow rose, trembling with dew; someone is asking us if we are all right.

She remarks that we are a real mess and she will have to find us something to wear home, we can't wear that dress. Again we experience confused images of the latter stages of the party, people sleeping in chairs, people trying to tidy up. The same voice says to 'try this on' and a huge, cobalt blue windcheater goes on over our head.

Our friend tells us to drop it in tomorrow because it's her brother's and it's new. We see the bundled wet dress thrust into our arms, we are asked if we are all right to get home. The voice adds, 'Just be bloody careful, walking alone.'

We are walking down badly lit streets when the heavens open and there is a torrential summer cloudburst. The streets are running with water and so are we. The rain is so heavy it is difficult to breathe. We get images of an ordinary redbrick house, the front gate, the sideway, the sleep-out and the bed. We flop. Darkness!

end Mungrel's bit

I think Mungrel told it better than this, but this is as close as I can get.

◉

Mungrel was smiling now, relieved. 'End of scene one. Your turn, Matt.' Mungrel grabbed his water bottle and topped up the billy that had been steaming away on the fire.

'So I make up the next bit?'

Mungrel nodded.

'Let me think.'

I told Becc who was sitting on my right, 'that Sheila kinda reminded me of someone else who got off her face'. She was really cut, you could tell, because she didn't say anything.

Matt cut in, 'Is this girl still at school?'

'Up to you, but I imagined her as being at school,' allowed Mungrel.

'She should have a dream,' Anna said.

'She'll have a hangover—dope and vodka!' Adam reckoned.

'But she threw up,' argued Dicko.

'Anyone is welcome to tell the next bit if Matt doesn't want it.' Mungrel was looking at Anna. 'You want to tell us the dream?'

'Can I, Matt? I don't think it would wreck whatever you would do . . .'

'Go for it, Anna. I'm not ready anyway. It's really hard to come up with that much of a story with no time.'

'You can do as much or as little as you like. Just a couple of images will do. When you do it properly you get lots of time,' Mungrel offered.

'Goanna!'

'Well, she has this dream,' Anna began. She didn't usually get this fired up, she always came across as being pretty straight, too mature for the rest of us. She always has the answers in class. She actually seems pleased to do well. When she frowns all her freckles join up. She hit me when she read that but I had to show her, I couldn't remember the details of her dream. They were too freaky so I had to ask her.

Anna's bit

In the dream she's making her deb and her dress won't stay white. She puts on this dress and goes to walk out to be presented and this rusty stain leeches through. So she takes it back and they wash it, she goes out again and the whole stain thing happens again, as soon as she walks out. She goes back again and this time it stains straight away so they spend a fortune to buy another dress.

But instead of wearing it she carries it in front of her and pretends that she is wearing it. Because she is not actually in it, it stays white but she spends her whole time whirling around in the dance so no one will see her rear view and the stained dress.

Then while she and her partner are waiting to be presented, these other couples keep appearing out of nowhere. They're like wild people. They're dressed in leaves and are near naked and they keep laughing and smiling and they just keep appearing, so she can't be presented. Eventually, she grabs her partner and barges into the line knocking everyone flying.

It takes her ages to walk up to the front so that, as she walks, she realises that the audience is largely naked, just sitting there like in 'The Emperor's New Clothes'. The bishop is naked and so is the principal. They look so foolish her sleazy-looking partner starts to laugh. He just loses it. He is on the floor wetting himself. She freaks out and gets so angry she starts to kick him. She knows she shouldn't but she can't help herself. As soon as she starts kicking there is blood everywhere and she wills herself awake.

She sits up in the night, feeling foul, doesn't even realise she is wet, crawls under the covers and goes back to sleep.

end Anna's bit

Anna looked around sheepishly, as if she might have revealed too much. She shrugged and tilted her head to look at Matt. 'I was worried she was going to get sick, I just had to get her under the covers. Over to you, Matt,' she offered.

I couldn't imagine Anna dreaming about kicking the hell out of someone, let alone doing it. Perhaps there was a head kicker inside Anna's subconscious—freaky!

'That was great, Anna!' Mungrel enthused. The others clapped lamely, more shocked than impressed. They were busy reassessing Anna, unsure that they had ever known her.

'Anna, where did this deb stuff come from?' Kelly asked the questions the others wanted to but weren't game. 'I thought you weren't going to do it.'

'I wasn't, I'm not, well at least I don't think I am, I mean it's all so absurd. We get dressed up like a bunch of virgins and get presented to a society that doesn't exist and if it did, wouldn't care if we stayed locked in our wardrobes. Coming out, what a stupid idea!'

The group had been talking about the deb ball flat-out for months and it wasn't until next year. I figured if the girls thought they didn't know Anna a few seconds before, now they knew her and they hated her. Mungrel's party games had turned to war.

'This hasn't got anything to do with the fact that you can't get a date, has it Anna?' God, Sarah could be a bitch. The claws were out; I was ready to run for cover.

'As a matter of fact...' it was Matthew wading in. I thought, you bloody idiot, the girls might treat you like a friend but don't get anywhere near them when they start to bitch; you start trying to calm things down, it's you they turn on. I'd like a dollar for every time I've heard a guy called an insensitive bastard. 'I offered to partner Anna.'

Again that gross silence when everyone mentally goes, 'What the...?' Now people were wondering if they knew Matt. Matt, what a legend, had blown them away. I thought I could lie, but this was inspired bullshit—even if the price was admitting to doing something very uncool with someone who was definitely un-chill. Anna and I have discussed the beautiful people since the camp.

But, this was Matt's specialty. He could actually make things cool. It was cool enough to get asked by a looker to do the deb thing with them, yet it was uncool to ask. Even if she had won the

English prize, being with Anna didn't win you any points. At least he'd saved Anna from the vultures.

'But you're partnering Cara.' Sarah couldn't leave it alone.

'Cara asked me after Anna had said no.' It seemed that it wasn't bullshit. Matt had actually done it. My only guess was that he felt sorry for her, but Anna would never stand for that. The worry was that he might actually be interested in her. Interested in her mind? They had been sitting next to each other in religious ed. Not only interested, but also willing to admit it in public. The bush seemed to be bringing out something strange in everybody.

'My bum's numb,' declared Steph.

'Billy's boiled,' announced Mungrel. 'Anyone for a cuppa?' He sprinkled tea-leaves into the boiling water. Big Bill Tuwhati, the other male teacher, was the only one who found a cup. He is a strange bloke. He never says much but you know he is watching and thinking. He is the only one, after the camp, that I still have no idea about.

'Yuck! What's that?' Yuck was Nancy's favourite word. Her mouth screws up like a cat's backside.

'Ah, er, I think it might be tea,' Adam was making sure someone pointed out the bleeding obvious.

'But how do you drink it with all those bits floating about free?'

'Nancy, dear!' Matt does a great snobby accent. 'We simply sieve it through our dentures, isn't that correct, Mr Mundle?'

Adam was doing the sound effects, gross slurping noises and then this beast slagging noise.

'Yuck!' he squeaked, really gay, like Nancy—pathetic really, but funny—then he slid to the ground in a faint.

Nancy and Marjorie looked at each other and stuck the boots in.

'Ladies please, no Romper Stomper in the kitchen! Grab a mug if you fancy a cuppa. Miss Tish might show you her trick with a Tim Tam.' Miss Tish looked a bit embarrassed.

'It's not my trick, it's yours, mine always get soggy and fall in.'

I figured that Mungrel and Miss Tish must have done a few camps together.

Miss Tish looked young enough to be his daughter, yet they got on pretty well. Someone told me later that Tish had actually gone to our school and Mungrel had taught her. I guess you would have to say Tish looks like a little Greek girl. She's tiny so we stand close to her and look down at her. The girls keep saying they want her hair, it's black, long and really curly, wild.

'What do you do with the choccy biscuit?' Kelly wanted to know.

'Well, it's a very delicate operation. I'll have to show you.' Mungrel headed for his pack. 'I don't think I've got enough for everyone.'

'I'd kill for a Tim Tam,' declared Kelly. 'Becc, you brought the marshmallows didn't you?'

'No, I thought you were going to...'

'It was your job,' accused Kelly.

'It's all right, you don't have to go sick, I brought three packets. Do you want me to get them? Don't just nod, say please.'

'Please, please, please get the marshmallows. Are they pink or white?'

Three marshmallows had been dropped in the fire and Dicko had burnt his mouth on one that was still alight (the dick) by the time Mungrel had poured the tea and was ready to give his demo.

Matt passed the pack around behind his back, not that Mungrel seemed to mind, but he was only going to get one go at his demonstration.

'Okay! You hold the cup of steaming beverage so! The Tim Tam so! You place the ends of the bickie in your mouth and nip off the end so! MMmm! You place the end of the bickie in the drink, wait until it starts to melt then... slurp... suck the tea through the bickie. So! The inside of the bickie melts as the tea goes past and you drink the biscuit, but you have to pop it into your mouth before it falls to pieces. Ah! Poo!' He was too slow; the soggy remains of the biscuit were floating around in his tea.

Most were happy to just fang into their biscuits without the risk of floaties.

'Are we gunna get to hear what happened to the girl at the party?' Becc was looking pointedly at Matthew.

'I'm not quite ready, it's really hard, I'm thinking though.'

Becc's bit

I can imagine her room if that's any help. Becc looked around for approval. *It's pale blue with this ugly old wardrobe along the wall near the door, there's one of those fold-up tables, square with skinny legs...*

'A card table,' Miss Tish offered.

Yeah, and this furry rug on the floor with a dog

on it and gross blue carpet underneath. There's one of those little rubbish bins made of wire; the only thing in it is this crumpled letter. The room's pretty bare, no posters or photos. The table is covered with books and homework stuff but apart from that it doesn't look like a teenager lives here—no makeup, no clothes all over the floor like Kell's. Her blazer is over the back of the chair but that's about all that shows a girl lives here.

She smiled shyly, great dimples. The firelight changes things. I remember thinking her ginger hair looked golden.

The bedcover is deep green with small splashes of orange, silver grey and brown. It's the only beautiful thing in the room. It looks like a sunset glimpsed through thick bush.

end Becc's bit

'Is the letter to her, or for somebody else?' Anna wanted to know.

'What letter?'

'The one in the bin.'

'Oh, I don't know, I thought it could have been one she'd written and then screwed up.'

'So why didn't she send it?' Anna was asking. She was way ahead of me.

Sarah ploughed in with, 'I reckon it was to her, from a guy, who dropped her.'

Becc was clear about this part. 'No! It's definitely a love letter, not a "you're dropped" letter.'

'Can I do the letter?' It was Miss Tish; she wanted to do the love letter. 'Do you want to do your bit, Matt? I don't mean to butt in.'

'Just jump right in, don't mind me, nobody else has! I had some ideas about half an hour ago but I've forgotten them it's been so long, so you go right ahead, feel free.' Matt was a bit pissed off.

'Well the crumpled letter in the bin is a love letter but it's also what Sarah suggested.'

'A "you're dropped" letter?' Sarah offered.

'Kind of. It says ... what's her name? Has she got one yet?' Miss Tish was looking at Mungrel.

'No one has given her one yet and we probably need to check if everyone is happy with our decision. It's usually good to leave things open, we might need to get to know her better,' Mungrel explained.

Tish's bit

Well, the letter says ... Miss Tish was staring into the flames. *Dear whoever, I wanted to say some-*

thing to you Sunday but you were too busy throwing coffee cups at me. Boy were you pissed off, I guess you still are. I guess I'll never get to show you the bruises.

We'd never heard Miss Tish swear before but she wasn't phased by our shock horror routine. She continued, staring into the fire, turning the torch in her hands in concentration.

I wish I could have been what you needed. I'm too young, too stupid, too dumb, too selfish. I don't know exactly.

There is a dark place in you. I always felt when we laughed and sang that we were really just holding back the dark. I wanted to ask, wanted to share the dark. But I was frightened. I wasn't sure I would like the black you, not sure I could cope if the darkness was in me, too.

I loved our time and laughter, our songs, I will never forget the feeling, dancing on the steps of the post office, lying in the sand with sunshine on our faces and in our hearts. I've never been so happy. It sounds really cliché, but... Miss Tish hesitated long enough to thrust her hands into the pocket of her fiberpile before continuing. Adam swung his big torch into the night and checked out the edge of the clearing.

'Thought I heard something,' he said.

'You scare us again and I'll beat the tripe out of you myself,' warned Kelly. Miss Tish was not distracted.

But . . . I know we're both in for dark days, cold days, chill and dismal days. There's just nothing I could do about it. I don't think you're likely to believe that, but it's the truth. If we hadn't been in love we could have been the best of friends. I really miss you even now.

I know you must hate me as only you can and know that no matter what I said, no reason for me ending it will ever make sense. I'm not sure myself but I just know you need more than I can give. You couldn't understand why I wouldn't make love with you; I wasn't ready, not for sex so much as ready for you. With you it would have been something irreversible, it would have changed everything. I'm not ready for what you needed. You always needed more from me than I was ready to give. I've got too much to learn myself; I want to be a kid. I don't want to be in love, even though I did, do love you. I feel guilty as hell, I think I have some idea of how much I hurt you and I'm not sure I'll ever forgive me. I don't expect you to.

I'll never forget our time. I can't be in love but I do love you. If I can help anytime, anywhere, call, I mean it, I'll be there. I'll leave you alone now. I hope we both find this joy again. I'm sorry for your pain, but I'm not sorry for our time.

Thank you.

Yours, the Bastard.

end Tish's bit

Miss Tish let out a big sigh and looked around challenging anyone to comment. No one was sure what we had just witnessed. This was not the boring maths teacher that they were used to.

I thought that for the first time we had seen something of the real Nina Tishlakis. No one was game to say anything except Mungrel.

'This quick try has turned into quite an epic already. This is great!'

'What a crock!' Steph exploded. 'Men make up such shit-full excuses for breaking it off! No offence, Miss Tishlakis, but that sounded like a crock. Bastard's right!'

The guys all made a mental note to steer clear of Steph.

Adam was waving his torch towards the edge of the clearing again when Becc started right in. 'I told you, Adam, you scare us again and...'

'I'm not kidding, I thought I heard something,' Adam pleaded.

'Shush!' whispered Sarah. 'I reckon I heard something, too.'

The group held its breath, listening to the fire and the darkness beyond. Seemed when we got quiet that the shadows crept closer to the fire.

'You are such a wanker, Adam!' Becc said.

'I wasn't kidding,' Adam muttered, as he stared out into the night. The wind had nearly dropped out by then. There was still the distant roar high above, where the tree tops cleared the protection of the gorge and were at the mercy of the wind. We listened to that mournful sound most of that night; sometimes it sounded more like a lost river than the wind in the trees.

Adam was holding the torch, slack-jawed, shitting himself. You could tell by the look on his face that he wasn't kidding. We followed the beam of his torch and there was the face.

Because the figure was all in dark colours it was hard to work out that it was a face. Because it was close to the ground the deep shadows and the strange angle made it look like a bunch of pale gum leaves in the light. But when you stared at it for a while it was like one of those visual puzzles—you can't see the face at first but after a minute you can make out the features. He must have thought he was invisible because he just sat there rock still. Until we started talking about him.

'It's a person!' squeaked Fei and that's when all hell broke loose. I still don't believe Mungrel asked him if he would like to join us for a cup of tea. Insane!

the sound
of whimpering

The thing I remembered on waking was the sound of whimpering. I'm not sure who was crying but someone was. I thought I was in a dream— what a dream! The pearly light creeping through the bush and my arms around Rebecca. I was in heaven. Nothing had happened, but I had Rebecca in my arms. She had really needed comforting so I had obliged. My arm felt like it had been amputated. I knew it would take some doing to wake it up now that Becc had been sleeping on it for hours. What a hero! I was wondering what had happened to Matt; I was supposed to share the tent with him.

After the face appeared, there was Fei's little scream, a few mutters from the others, but then there was silence. He looked at us and we looked at him. We waited for him to answer our questions, spoken and unspoken, but he stood and stared at us. In the torchlight his ghostly face reflected the colours of the fire. He was dressed in loose-fitting dark clothes so that the face appeared to float in the shadows. He was standing now. His hair had been roughly cropped short, and his face was the colour of yellow clay—in fact I realised the face was daubed with yellow ochre that made it look like a mask. The thing that really got me were the eyes. They were huge. Perhaps it was the clay, but they were like the eyes of a rabbit caught in headlights, unblinking, bewildered and vulnerable. But there was also an intensity about them that scared me. From that first glimpse I knew this guy was crazy. He didn't care about anything. He was staring at us and I felt his hate roll over me like a chill damp cloud. I felt like I shouldn't have been there. I was invading his world. Others said they couldn't look at his eyes, they were too frightening. Maybe we were just scared and we imagined the rest.

There were lots of questions racing through my mind. What was someone doing ten Ks from the road with no gear? What sort of person wandered about in the bush on his own? What did he want? Why didn't he answer when Mungrel spoke to him? How long had he been there? Where did he come from? Why did he creep up on us? Who was he? Not, was he dangerous, but how dangerous was he? We waited for him to say, 'Hi, sorry to freak you out, just mucking around.' But he didn't, and you could tell from his eyes that he wasn't going to. Why have you painted your face with clay? Where did you escape from? How many people have you killed? Why do you have to freak us out?

Big Bill, Mr Tuwhati, stepped around the fire and spoke into the taut silence. 'What's ya name…? Can we help you with something…? Listen, you shouldn't freak people out.'

Big Bill took a step forward and the spell was broken. The face turned and he bounded straight into the bush. He didn't use the track. There was a broad area beside the river where those thorn bushes with fine, two-centimetre-long thorns had grown into a wall. We had been skirting around their nasty spikes since we arrived. They were really nasty; the points stuck in then broke off. He just lifted his arms to cover his face and ran straight at them. He knew that they were there. He'd had to crawl through them to creep up on us.

We were glad to see him go but we hadn't had our questions answered, so we answered them for ourselves. The person who wanders around the bush with no gear and a painted face and creeps up on unsuspecting campers is a big-time loony who stalks people to cut their throats in the night or chop them into little pieces and throw their limbs down mineshafts.

We all went spazmoid. Some were crying, others stunned. I was stunned; I lost it. I wanted to be home, wanted to be anywhere else.

Big Bill was the third teacher., He's pretty strict and most of us are fairly scared of him. He's got a reputation with our parents. He taught most of them and they're still scared of him. I don't care how big he is, he's braver than I am— there's no way I'd have had the guts to go off into the dark. It was full-on dark; the clouds just soaked up all the light. Big Bill walked over to Nancy, took her torch and said to Mungrel. 'I'll just make sure he keeps going. I don't think we need him hanging around.' He was being very calm. He moved to head off.

'He's probably just an eccentric, lives local maybe,' Mungrel offered.

'I wish. Very eccentric. Very strange. I won't be long.'

'Okay.' Mungrel lowered his voice but we all heard. 'Um, you got a knife or a stick or something?'

Big Bill nodded, patted his pocket and headed up the track that led back along the river.

I wondered if Big Bill had seen those eyes clearly. He must have, he was closer to him than the rest of us. I remembered where I had seen that yellow clay mask before. It was what they wear in New Guinea. I remember seeing them milling around on TV with their faces covered in mud. But those eyes were too big, too wild, too haunted, too deranged. I would not have been going out into the night with him out there. I still felt the chill wave of hate.

I was paralysed. I was grateful no one expected anything of me. I was glad that it was up to the teachers; I could be a kid. When you run into a pack playing footy it takes physical courage. I could do that. But for the first time I didn't want to be out there, I wanted to be home.

The bush that had felt peaceful a few minutes ago as we sat around the fire was now filled with noises and it was watching.

It was far worse than a ghost story. It was real. Ghost stories were just fun, playing with being scared. When that guy with the yellow face, whoever he was, took off into the scrub there was this sinking feeling. The only time I felt like this was when I first heard about one of those mass-murders, where some freak took a gun and just shot heaps of innocent people.

Most of us had never really been scared before. We'd all had childish fears, bad dreams, and been scared on some carnival ride, but then it was controlled fear—we woke up or the ride finished. We were starting to wake up, but the nightmare was still going. I think it was Nancy crying that she wanted to go home but she was not the only one. There was no shame. I think crying was what we all felt like doing.

We'd all expected this guy to just walk into the firelight and tell us who he was and everything would be normal. We were shocked, in shock I guess. Mungrel was so cool, 'come in for a cuppa,' he'd called; that was either stupid or very cool. But this bastard just took off into those prickle bushes; he wasn't mucking about, ploughed straight through them. He would be pulling thorns out of his skin for days. As time went by it became obvious that someone's brother wouldn't walk out of the scrub and say it was all a joke.

Big Bill had been away too long. He'd gone down the track closest to the direction the guy had taken—the prickle bushes were impossible to get through. It was not some practical joke. And Big Bill sure wasn't known for his sense of humour. We were a full day's walk from anywhere and we were alone. Big Bill was a big bastard and Mungrel could probably hold his own if he had to fight, but we were isolated. Big Bill hadn't come back. If he were gone or dead what would stop this mad bastard from killing us all? We felt really vulnerable knowing that whoever it was had been able to just sit there in the dark, watching and listening to us. I'm not sure why that last part upset me, but it really did. It wasn't just the fear, it was the outrage, the invasion, that made you feel like tears.

We didn't know how long he'd been there and we didn't know why. I think most of us were already thinking about him as the axe-murderer. I just kept seeing that staring yellow face, that death's head, that hunted, haunted look.

While everyone was going troppo Mungrel and Miss Tish were just happy if we stayed calm, so they weren't fussed if we were comforting each other. There wasn't much conversation, just some lame jokes about axe-murderers. We didn't want to leave the fire, but eventually it got cold and I'm sure Mungrel was worried about Big Bill so he chased us off to bed. Rebecca had curled up at my feet while we were still around the fire. I'd put a hand on her shoulder and she'd eventually ended up sitting on my lap. Kelly was already on Matt's lap, so no one seemed to notice. When Mungrel sent us to bed at two a.m. because we were half asleep already, Becc didn't want to go to her own tent so she just tagged along with me. No one seemed to mind; we were just comforting each other. Shame was, we just fell asleep—must have been shock or something. I figured Matt must have been in with Kelly, Becc's tent mate. I hoped so anyway.

When I woke I could see out the end of the tent. We hadn't wanted to zip it up; we hadn't discussed it, it just seemed too easy for someone to sneak up on you if the tent was closed. The clearing looked unreal; there was this mist so everything looked transparent. Mungrel was sitting on a log. He looked like he was asleep. He was rugged up so I guessed he'd been there all night. He fitted into the scene like one of those pioneer paintings, misty, serene. His presence and the light made me forget about the axe-murderer.

I felt a bit guilty. He'd been guarding the fort all night, and I'd been curled up with Becca. Making time. Big Bill wasn't back and I didn't know what to make of that. If Mungrel had stayed awake all night, there was something to worry about. But for now I could smell Rebecca's breath as she slept. It was really sweet like she'd been eating musk sticks; my breath smells like the bottom of a cockatoo's cage. She was one sweet pants. What do you do when the world is ending? You grab the best looking piece of ass and get cosy. Sorry Becc!

I must have gone back to sleep because the next time I woke up Becc was eating cornflakes over at the fire. I felt a bit cheated that she'd escaped, but the truth was there was no way I was going to get to first base after last night. It had been a good start; at least I could say I'd slept with Rebecca. In my dreams!

We were a bit sleepy and the whole place seemed a bit unreal. Dicko even started picking up sleeping bags to see if the axe-murderer was underneath. Just in case we were in any doubt about what happened the night before, the teachers reminded us. Sarah and Nancy were heading off to go to the toilet. They told them they weren't allowed. The girls started pleading and whingeing. 'Don't go too far,' Miss Tish said in the end.

They were back so fast you expected to see a trail of toilet paper following them back. Adam asked them if they buried it deep. 'Don't want it following us all the way to the next campsite,' he commented.

'Enough of that toilet humour, thank you, Adam. It's time you got packed up. Some people have already taken their tents down.'

The only ones that had in fact taken their tent down were the teachers. They had taken one down but it seemed they hadn't made up their minds. Big Bill's pack was still there, and they didn't seem to know what to do about it. Miss Tish and Mungrel had this whispered conference. The obvious thing would have been for Mungrel to have a look for him; he seemed to know his way around. He had actually snuck down the track a couple of hundred metres but come back. I guess now that he didn't want to leave us alone, and I know it didn't seem to make much sense for another teacher to head off. I guess they saw their responsibility as looking after us because they herded us together, got us organised and did a count. Mungrel said later that leaving Big Bill out there on his own was one of the worst moments of the week. Mungrel took the mobile phone out of Big Bill's pack and left him a note.

A few of the kids had been quietly making comments to each other when Adam opened his trap. 'Why don't we just wait for Mr Tuwhati? Don't ya reckon he's gunna come back?'

Mungrel looked at Miss Tish. 'I'm not sure at this stage what to expect, I'm worried about Mr Tuwhati and . . .'

'The axe-murderer,' interjected Adam.

'And whoever else is out there.' Adam was getting the greasiest looks from Mungrel. 'But the first thing I intend to do is get you guys up to the road so I can use the phone and get some help in here to find out what's going on. What I don't need at the moment is too many comments, understood?'

Most understood; Mungrel didn't get too heavy, too often. But I think Adam was scared. He wouldn't shut up. 'Why don't you just run up to the top of the ridge with the phone and we can wait for Big Bill?'

It was a reasonable question but I think the teachers had already thought about it and didn't want us left with just Miss Tish.

'Just pick up your pack and shut up.'

That's when we realised how scared the teachers were. I noticed later that Miss Tish and Mungrel had picked up sticks to use as walking sticks. Adam, Matt and I did too, which turned out to be a good idea as the next stretch along the river was really steep. Mungrel got Matt and me to walk behind Miss Tish at the front and he followed at the back of the group, sometimes dropping back—I guess to make sure there was nobody following.

The country changed, the track itself was less defined, and we were further from civilisation than most walkers go. The gorge gets wider so that although the river is never far away we were able to spread out a bit. We were able to get the odd glimpse of the river silvering its way south and see more sky then we had since we started down the river. It would have been beautiful apart from the cloud of fear we carried; the noise the wallabies made bounding away into the bush sounded like our hearts.

It was a pretty tense morning; the girls were all bunched together and quiet as. Dicko and Adam were bullshitting as usual, talking about computer games, guns and cars. They always talk about the same stuff; neither of them has a gun or a car but if you listen to them you'd think they were hot-rod Rambos. The only thing that finally shut them up was the cracking pace Miss Tish was setting. She was sweating and she'd obviously made up her mind we were going to break some kind of a record heading up the Razorback. She was hammering along so that by the first stop we were all panting.

The packs were bloody heavy and even though the sun was too low to reach us, we were hot. We were dressed for sitting around in the morning chill. We broke out the water. It was nice to have a couple of kilometres between our first campsite and us; we began to relax a little.

The scrub was thinner where the track came back to the river so we cheered up and peeled off the layers. It was a relief to be out of that heavier scrub. We could see much further. It was harder for someone to get close without us seeing him. Lots of people must have been holding out to go to the toilet. One of the girls said she was going and she ended up with nine friends. They marched off into the scrub—strength in numbers. I just hoped they were far enough from the track.

While the rest of us were trying not to shit ourselves, literally, and looking over our shoulders for axe-murderers, Matt had been busy. It seems this epic idea had got hold of his brain and he'd been thinking about his part of the story all morning, so when he launched into it at our morning stop, we didn't know at first what he was talking about. I don't know why I assumed the epic could only be told around the fire, but I was surprised when Matt launched into it, perched on a log in full sunshine.

Matt's bit

She is blue from her knees to her ears. It is the blue of dead bodies but brighter, like twilight skies. She rubs condensation from the mirror and tries to remember; she is not quite awake. As usual she is in the shower before she is conscious; she looks now and sees the deep blue windcheater in the laundry basket. She has slept in her clothes often enough but can't remember where the top came from. She remembers part of the trip home in the pouring rain and little else. She realises that she has gone to bed wet and her skin colour is the result of the dye running from the windcheater. She feels fuzzy in the head and realises it is probably the dope still in her system.

She smiles now. It is comical, to think that she has slept at least part of the night with the wet, blue windcheater top over her nose so that the blue line across her face is quite distinct. It would be funny if she didn't have to go to school or face the olds for breakfast. Where was she supposed to be last night, whose place had she told them she was going to? Homework at Claire's, that's the best alibi. Claire's Mum is such a pain that her folks would never ring in case they end up on the phone for hours.

She runs her tongue around her mouth and vaguely remembers throwing up on the lawn; the memories are coloured by the desperation with which she'd wiped herself out. It is a little embarrassing—straight vodka and dope, not very dignified. She remembers the letter in the bin and forgets the amusing side of being blue; she half groans like she has been hit, by pain, ambushed by the memory. Now she is really blue. The thought that she has to face the folks over breakfast rankles; she just doesn't feel like a fight.

She need not have worried. They are both on their way out the door. She waits until they go, turns off 3LO and the depressing news and puts on Triple J. She is living two lives, the one from the party last night and the one her parents and teachers see.

She begins going through the motions of getting ready for school, putting her hair up because that is what is expected at school; it's all automatic; she realises that she does very little by choice, mostly she operates as she is expected to. Although she is appalled by the idea, she just keeps getting ready for school. She even has another shower to try and get more of the blue off. She is going to use some cover up makeup but decides that she looks like something from the jungles of South America. This is the first minor rebellion for the day. It might even catch on, she thinks. Now that would be something. There is no rule against blue skin; she knows this from writing out the school rules in detention. She drags the pile of

untouched books back into her bag, thinks about put-
ting her blazer on but stuffs it into the bag as well.
She closes the gate carefully and turns to look at the
house. It's one of those red brick places that have lead-
light windows, but the blinds are drawn. It looks like
it has closed its eyes. She gives it the finger and heads
off to the bus.

Matt looked across at Kelly and brushed the corkscrew of red curls off his forehead. It was common knowledge that they had ended up together the night before. I decided to ask Matt later if they had shared more than the tent. I didn't expect that he would tell me; he is like that. His look at Kelly was like saying, 'stick with me', apologising in advance as if the next part of the story might upset her. Matt took a deep breath and continued.

By the time she gets close to the bus stop, whatever
has made her angry at home now makes her furious.
She isn't just angry with her folks; she is angry with
herself for going to school, for wearing the uniform, for
being so ordinary, so good. She is angry at the sun for
shining. She turns the corner of the street and there is
Courtney. Courtney is the boyfriend.

He is still a long way off but she can tell it is him by
the way he stands there with the bag over his shoulder.
There is something loose and casual about the way he

moves—normally she thinks it cool, now it seems a pose. He is playing those pathetic games that all her friends play.

They ended up going out, she now realises as she walks towards him, because her friends thought that they would make a good couple. He's cute, she's pretty enough; the others probably think they look like a couple out of 'Neighbours' or 'Home and Away'.

They are the clean-cut couple. Where is the romance, she asks herself, it is more like a business deal. I'll be your boyfriend, so that everyone will know that we are going out with someone. That we are desirable, straight. That we belong. Courtney is okay, he isn't a prick, he treats her all right, sits with her on the bus, hangs out most of the time but she is sure he'd much rather be kicking the footy with his mates.

She isn't angry with him. She is angry with her friends for wasting their time. It is going nowhere. Wearily she realises she'll have to end it, the sooner the better, but not on the bus—that would be a bit public.

She is surprised then when he speaks first. 'I tried to ring you last night. You said that you'd be there.' It was all a blur. She felt yesterday was forever ago, last night was a dream. She looked down at her blue wrists.

'When did I say that?'

'Yesterday, on the bus.'

She realises he is peeved about something. Perhaps he will break it off, she thinks hopefully. 'I'm sorry I wasn't there, I forgot, what did you want anyway?'

'I just rang, that's what ya do when you're going out, isn't it? Where were you anyway?'

'I went to Tossa's party, as a matter of a fact. You said that you didn't want to go.'

'You didn't tell me you were going to go anyway.'

'You said you didn't want to go where everyone would be off their faces and pretending to be hippies. Are you pissed off with me because I went?'

Courtney is looking sheepish now.

'We're supposed to be going out, what are people going to think if you go to parties without me?'

'I don't give a fuck what people think! I'm sorry I damaged your reputation last night, arriving alone, getting stoned, screwing around, throwing up on the front lawn— maybe you'd better find yourself another girlfriend.'

She stands there fuming as the bus rolls up. She isn't sure this is really happening; this is one strange day. She sits in her usual seat while Courtney heads down the back with the back-seat toughs. She has her usual smoke and then lights another. She is shocked by how quickly things change. For the first time in her life she realises anything could happen, she can make it *happen, there is an adventure out there and it's a choose-your-own ending.*

She is about to shove her smokes back into her bag but then lights another and walks off the bus, in uniform, out the front of the school, past the teacher talking to some kid about not wearing their blazer—she is not wearing hers. She is tingling; she feels like she is in a trance; the girl from the party has come to school. She casually finishes the smoke as she walks up the stairs to her classroom, butts it on the step and walks inside. Perhaps it is because she is so casual that none of the school staff notice. The kids around her walking from the bus are dumbfounded. They can't believe that anyone can be so obvious and not get caught.

She doesn't feel anything, no real excitement. She has made her choice, she is prepared to take what is coming. If anything she is pissed off that all this time she has been petrified about getting caught. Now she has smoked her way across the schoolyard and into the building and there are no consequences. She decides that at least until lunchtime she will go with the flow. Besides, all her friends are hanging out to talk about the party and some have heard already that she has dropped Courtney at the bus stop. At least the morning will be fun. Then Tanya screams, 'Ahh! You're all blue!'

end Matt's bit

Matt pulled a plastic bag out of his pack 'Scrotum, anyone?'

'Scroggin, Matt!' Mungrel like everyone else was listening to Matt's part of the epic. We hadn't realised that he had finished.

'What's scroggin?' asked Adam

Mungrel looked to see if the question was serious or a send up as was usual with Adam. 'It's a collection of fruits, seeds and nuts specifically for bush walking. Not unlike you guys.

'What is?' asked Adam.

'Scroggin!' supplied Kelly

'I was saying that you guys were an interesting mix of fruits and nuts, but I rest my case. Matt, pass the scrotum and then I think we better get a move on. In case you guys have forgotten we are still short a teacher. Saddle up and let's make like a tree and leaf.'

We were walking again before we had time to think. We had been away in Matt's story; we had forgotten the situation we were involved in. The thing that occurred to me as we started winding away from the river again was that the normal world of the epic seemed more real than the bush walk. The girl on the bus was our normal world. This camp seemed like a dream, a nightmare; the crazy yella fella in the bush last night, the unreality of the teacher missing in action, presumed dead. No one presumed anything yet but we'd all thought about it. Matt's story had been a nice escape.

The other interesting idea was that we were all more relaxed. The guy had interrupted the epic last night, scared shit out us, so that all we could think about was him. Now Matt had made us forget about him for a few minutes. He'd pinched back the story that was stolen from us. We all felt it; we just sorta sighed and relaxed a bit. We'd been on the edge of panic. We weren't sure you could actually cope with this sort of tension; we'd never been this vulnerable before. Matt in telling the story had made us feel that we could still be in control. We were together and could choose not to be frightened, at least not frightened out of our gourd. What's a gourd?

Two thoughts on the one day! That guy in the bush really made me think. But then since the girls weren't walking huddled together I stopped thinking and talked to Becca. I thought it was a good idea to remind her how terrific I was last night, but all she wanted to talk about was how brave Big Bill had been. To just walk out into the bush not knowing what was out there was just plain brave. I reminded her that Big Bill was 110 kilos, heaps bigger than the guy we had seen, looked like he'd escaped from the film *Once Were Warriors* and was the sole reason we no longer challenged the staff to football matches. The staff call him Twinkletoes when they play footy. I don't understand; he plays more like the Bendigo express. If you're between him and his destination you're road kill. I think I was just jealous, jealous of the way she talked about him. Becc was sure she would never do it. I wondered if I was older and it was my job whether I would have. I decided I would have been like Mungrel—just a bit shocked, not ready to tear off into the bush, not petrified but just surprised. No way I would've asked them if they wanted a cup of tea, though. It was as though Mungrel never imagined someone would act like that and Big Bill was expecting him to do exactly what he did.

They were pretty different guys, though. Big Bill was phys ed and Mungrel was mainly drama–English. They were both okay teachers but we were thinking about them as men now. They had lives outside school; they had histories.

'Why would anyone want to become a teacher when they get so much shit?' I asked Becc. She said she had wanted to be a teacher when she was in primary school. I thought, right! She's a suck, the teachers really like her, she's pretty, smart and she does all the right things—she even gets to do Tournament of Minds. What was I doing trying to crack onto her? She was too good for me.

I laughed at that idea and then couldn't explain what I was laughing at. She told me she had this teacher who read them really good picture storybooks and she wanted to do that. She even confided that she still loved being read to. I imagined reading stories to her in her bedroom. She interrupted my daydream by asking me didn't I just love the epic, especially Matt's bit and who did the girl remind me of. I had no idea. I felt I knew the girl but she didn't remind me of anyone in particular; she was just like lots of girls.

She asked Tanja then and they were off bitchin' about their friends and enemies while I avoided boredom by looking behind bushes for axe-murderers. I decided to do everyone a favour and find out from Matt who the girl was. I dropped back to where Matt was walking with Kelly and asked him. He didn't answer for a minute and then told Kelly that it wasn't her. 'It's based on real people but it's not really anyone. It's someone new, built on lots of old. The guy, the boyfriend, he's based on someone but I'm not telling who.' I found myself wondering if it was me; I had this thought that maybe I treated girls like that, but it wasn't me. I never got that jealous. I would have split before things got that uncomfortable. Too scared maybe, I don't want to get dropped. I wondered.

I'm not scared of spiders and snakes or horror movies or running into the ruckman from Melton. Blokes aren't supposed to get scared but then I remembered that minute of panic when I thought I was lost, that freaked me. Then there was that yella fella in the firelight; I now understand how people really do wet themselves when they are really scared; that would be gross. Now I had discovered that I'm scared of girls, not girls but I guess you'd call it rejection. Here I am lusting after Becc and I think she is interested too but now I realise I'm worried that she might tell me to piss off. I thought about Big Bill and Mungrel. They were pretty brave last night. How do you get to be a real man?

Matt was talking about this book he was reading, called *Holding the Man*. I thought it was a footy book but it turns out that it's about these two gay guys. Matt says it goes into real detail about what they do with each other. 'Shit! How gross!' That was Kelly and I had to agree. But Matt reckons it's really, really sad, it's a real love story. I said they'd probably both die of AIDS; he said they did.

He's strange Matt, he reads all sorts of strange stuff. I guess that's why he can make up great stories. I asked him what was going to happen next. He said he didn't know and that it was someone else's turn to tell the next part of the story.

I decided to do a survey. I thought it might take people's mind off the axe-murderer. I dropped back to where Mungrel was bringing up the rear. He looked worried so I asked Steph. She started by telling me she had no idea, then told me she thought the girl in the story was going to get into trouble. She would probably tell someone where to go. That sounded like Steph to me. Maybe we all imagine ourselves into stories—I'd just been wondering if the guy was me.

We had been skirting the ridge above the river, only catching glimpses of it occasionally. It was difficult to walk two abreast; I had to stop my survey. The bush here was quite thick and crowded the track so that you could only see the backside of the person in front of you. I realised that everyone had stopped talking and stayed quite close to the one in front of them. I was kind of pleased to have Mungrel behind me, although if he disappeared as he seemed to every so often, I was the next one to get it in the neck. Marjorie was the one in front of Steph. There was no sign of her flaking out. She wasn't looking for attention; she was just as keen as the rest of us to get out of that gorge. In fact no one had complained about their pack, the track, the lack of toilets, nothing. The ochre yella axe-murderer with the huge eyes had made us realise that we were reliant on ourselves and each other. This was exactly what the camp coordinator had been on about when he tried to convince us to go on the camp. God I hate it when teachers are right; thank God it don't happen too often.

I think people were pretty anxious about slipping down the slope. No one liked the idea of spraining an ankle. The plan was to lunch at the bottom of Spanish Onion Track, cross the river and head up the Razorback Track. Once we were up onto the shoulder of the gorge the phone would work and the four-wheel drive would be able to ferry us out if necessary. Mungrel and Miss Tish seemed concerned about the fact that we were one teacher short. I think the emergency plans said you couldn't leave the group with one staff member.

If Mungrel was to go looking for Big Bill he couldn't leave the group with Miss Tish. I don't think she would have been too keen on being left on her own anyway. I wasn't sure what Mungrel and Miss Tish were thinking, but I know I would have been calling the cops.

As it turned out they didn't have a choice. We stopped for lunch at the river crossing. The river was cheerful, the water babbling over the stones. It was good to be out of the dim sameness of the bush. The sun even came out for a few minutes. Again we felt much safer where we could see each other and it would be hard to sneak up on us.

'Whose turn for the epic?' asked Mungrel as we got comfy for lunch on the logs and rocks beside the shallows. 'Matt's kept us pretty realistic; it doesn't have to stay that way. Anyone got something?'

Dicko's bit

There's this truck... Everyone groaned. It was Dicko. He always started with this truck. His mouth was full of uncooked two minute noodles.

'It's a Kenworth Linemaster,' continued Adam, sending Dicko up further.

'Yeah!' agreed Dicko. 'It's red and white with bits of kangaroo hanging off the bull-bar.'

'That's gross!' objected most of the girls. Dicko was smiling wildly. He loved this.

'What's this got to do with the girl?' asked Kelly patiently.

'What girl? He's talking about a truck.' Adam doesn't handle too many changes in direction.

Thankfully, Kelly was her patient self; that's probably why people like her, she's not a suck, just a soft touch. She began to explain. 'The girl in the story, the blue one who just broke up with her boyfriend…'

'And smoked a joint on the way into school.' Adam was back on track, it was just the details he was foggy on.

'It was a cigarette, Adam. We were just wondering if Dicko's truck fits in with the story.'

'I'm glad you asked that, Kelly. You see, if you let me finish, I'm about to introduce the enigmatic stranger.'

Mungrel choked in a fit of laughter.

Dicko looked a bit doubtful. 'Yeah the enigmatic drifter like Clint Eastwood. He don't say much but he sorts it. That's right, ain't it, enigmatic? He don't talk, he just has this look as if he understands everything, although no one understands him.'

Mungrel looked impressed now that he had

swallowed his dry biscuit and his fit of laughter. 'Enigmatic is indeed the correct word.'

Well this fat truck driver... Dicko was confident now.

'Sounds like your dad.' That was Adam.

'Yeah, except this time he's sober,' Dicko greased a grin at Adam.

... He sees this guy ten Ks east of Ceduna, heading across the Nullarbor on foot. It's forty-six degrees outside the air-conditioned cab. He knows this guy ain't gunna make it on foot. He pulls the truck off the bitumen into the bull dust. He waits for the guy to jump in but he doesn't even look around. He peeps the air-horn; the guy jumps but doesn't turn around. He can see the guy has a bottle of water but he knows in weather like this a litre of water won't last him till smoko. He swears because he hates getting his fat arse out of the truck and this guy is a serious fruitcake. But there is a code of the highway and truckies won't leave you to rot.

He grabs the guy's swag. 'You'll die out here. This heat'll kill ya.' The guy is hanging onto the cord that holds the swag around his shoulder just looking at the truckie as if he can't understand a word he's saying. The truckie's met some foreign hitch-hikers who don't speak English before and reckons this guy is one, so instead of trying to talk to him, he points to the truck and drags the guy and his swag towards the cabin. The

guy sees the paw of the wallaby on the bull-bar and
stares. The truckie snatches the swag from him throws
it up into the cabin, climbs over to his side and slips it
into gear. He waits forever as the guy climbs up into
the cabin and grabs the swag. He drops the clutch and
they're headed for Port Augusta. The truckie smiles at
him to put him at ease, and says again, 'You were
gunna die out there.' The guy just holds his swag and
stares out into the glare.

end Dicko's bit

Dicko had finished; this doesn't sound like Dicko's
style but when I asked him later he couldn't even
remember what he'd said in his bit.

Anna wanted more. 'Apart from the fact that
he doesn't talk, what does this guy look like? Just
in case we meet him somewhere further into the
epic, does he have to? Talk, I mean. What happens
if we forget someone?'

Dicko knew what he looked like. 'He's just
ordinary, blue eyes, brown hair, tanned skin, fit,
looks like he knows how to work. He's got this tattoo on his forehead; it's sort of bluish and it looks
like a lizard, a gecko.' Dicko picked up a stick and
drew a stick-figure lizard in the river sand. It only
had three legs. 'That's what he looks like.'

'We could do an epic just explaining where the guy and his scar comes from,' muttered Mungrel.

'It's a tattoo,' insisted Dicko.

'Tattoo,' agreed Mungrel, as he got up and asked if anyone needed tape on their hot-spots. He explained that we were going to head up the Razorback and it would be tough going for the first hour or so. The hill meant that hot-spots on your feet would quickly become blisters.

It wasn't part of the original plan to climb the ridge, but at least the four-wheel drive would be able to get to us at the top, if the phone worked. Again it felt like a dream to leave the story and get back into the real world. I think everyone would have preferred just to sit there in the afternoon sun, telling stories. There was too much un-certainty and fear in the real world. We were fart-ing around changing socks and finishing lunch, despite Mungrel's instructions to get going.

He cracked. 'Mr Tuwhati doesn't need to spend another night out here without help. Now shift your backsides.'

We hammered up the first part of the track, which was pretty dumb, because Marjorie flaked out and actually rolled down the slope. She wasn't faking it—she was out to it. We were climbing a long spur that angles up from the river, gently at first but the higher you get the steeper it becomes and finally you follow along the spine of the razorback. We sat on this steep scrubby track where we were stuck in single file while Miss Tish and Mungrel tried to bring Marj around.

Steph was above me on the track and Sarah was below, Sarah had been pretty quiet since all this stuff started, she is usually the first one to start bellyaching. 'We have to climb that, you have got to be joking, we didn't pay a hundred and twenty bucks to be tortured.' Like I said she'd been really quiet. I listened to her ask Steph about her asthma, I wondered if she was quiet because she was scared or because she wasn't the wuss we thought she was.

I noticed Steph was wheezing quietly and had to take a deep breath each time she answered. Sarah was asking questions about her breathing and medication, not just idle questions; she was working out the best way to help get Steph to the top of the hill. It seems Sarah has a younger sister who is a bad asthmatic. It was interesting that neither of them had told the teachers. When the going gets tough . . . the bitch, it seems, gets going. I started to think about if there was any way I could help.

It became clear pretty quickly that we weren't meant to get to the top of this hill. Marjorie stood up and promptly slid to the ground again. As she slid to the ground so did our hopes. When Mungrel turned us around and headed back to the river, we knew we were in for another night in the gorge. We were herded slowly downstream, Mungrel nearly carrying Marjorie, to a broader, open area where we could spread out and at a pinch, pitch tents. Mungrel was fiercely calm. There was an intensity about the way he settled Marjorie and organised us to collect wood in pairs. I had the impression that if someone got hysterical he'd nuke'em with a look. This camp was not supposed to go like this. Things were not going to plan and the emergency plans had just fallen to pieces. We'd seen them when we did our planning. There was nothing about muddy axe-murderers and lost teachers. You could feel the panic in the air. People obeyed without question, happy just to be busy. There were a couple of hours of light left, but the sun was over the hill We were going to be in shadow pretty soon.

Mungrel called us together and told us he was going to run up the hill and see if he could get the phone to work. Meanwhile he wanted no one to leave the camp, keep the fire going and keep a couple of big sticks handy. He asked us, without going silly just to make sure there were no visitors. I just stood there; Mungel was going to leave us with Miss Tish. She is so little I could've picked her up and thrown her across the river. I wasn't feeling very comfortable. He said he hoped to be back before dark. I think we were all on the edge of panic again. I think he saw the fear in my eyes because he put a hand on my shoulder as he walked past. 'You'll be right.' Fourteen kids and one midget maths teacher, another teacher missing in action, now the other adult was taking off. We told ourselves he would be back before dark and got busy making ourselves useful.

Mungrel grabbed the phone, his torch, coat, map, and Adam, then headed up the hill. Adam, carrying the biggest torch I'd ever seen, looked very serious and important as he headed up the Razorback. I wondered if it was the fact that he was strong and fit from footy, or that he was the one most likely to do something dumb while Mungrel was away, that led to his selection. Some of the girls were as fit as Matt; Nancy is the best distance runner in our year. He should have taken me as it turned out. I wouldn't have been all that keen. We had only just started the climb that afternoon and I'd been buggered. Mungrel was just going to run up the hill to see if the phone worked, sure!

Miss Tish came over and told us to make sure that there was a tent for Mungrel and Adam as they might get back in the dark. We were well ahead of her. There was a spare tent as I said I'd bunk in with Dicko and Matt. It would be a bit of a squeeze but there wasn't much room for extra tents on the rocky elbow of the river. I was hoping it wouldn't rain or we could all be sharing a rather cool bath.

Put people under pressure and it's amazing how they react. I thought that left alone, Miss Tish might freak out. I know Mungrel didn't want to leave her alone but it was like she was just waiting for Mungrel to get out of the way. She made decisions, but best of all she was really funny. She started telling us to form a circle with the tents, in case of attack from redskins or Maoris—Mr Whati is actually Maori. Then she started sending up Mungrel, 'You men there, get a big stick and protect these poor helpless women. Back in the jungle for two days and these men turn into apes.' I did feel a bit foolish standing there with half a gum tree.

Somehow the girls decided to do a shuffle. Kelly, Becc and Nancy moved in together. They were best mates at kinder. Steph and Sarah were sharing. By the time we had eaten, organised our tents and collected enough wood to keep the fire going for three weeks it was dark. We'd expected Mungrel back before dark, ideally with a gang of cops to start looking for Big Bill and find the arsehole who'd frightened hell out of us.

The last light had leeched from the sky. We were all seated around the fire trying flat out not to flash the torches at the shadows. We felt a bit more secure because we had camped on a spit or elbow at the bend of the river; this meant we had water on two out of three sides. The drawback was that we couldn't hear anything above the sound of the river. It sounded like a carnival—you could imagine distant voices, jangly music, and I swear I could hear a steam engine. We were talking real loud. We'd talked about little else besides our situation since it began. Now we were trying to talk about anything but. We tried especially hard not to think about Big Bill. When there is something you want to avoid talking about, it's the only thing that comes into your mind.

But we were all thinking the same sort of thing. 'Where would you like to be right now?' It was Nancy's question.

'Paris.' It was Miss Tish and the answer was automatic. 'Or Florence maybe,' she added.

'Home, watching… what time is it? Home watching telly. Tuesday night is soapie night.' Sarah hadn't hesitated.

'I have absolutely no idea.' It was Anna. 'I usually say, right where I am, but I can think of a few places I would rather be, anywhere safe. This is nice, a beautiful place, I'd just like to feel safe and normal.'

Most agreed that the camp would have been okay if things had gone to plan.

Anna's second bit

'The blue girl in the third row will please pay attention.' The other students sniggered. She looked up at the writing on the whiteboard. It seemed to say nothing; there were words but they did not penetrate. She had grown tired of painting by numbers. Everyone had changed the language they were using but no one had thought to tell her. She was adrift in a foreign country. She was an alien. She no longer belonged.

'What's painting by numbers?' Sarah asked. Most were now aware that the next episode of the epic had begun.

Some had assumed that you couldn't do the epic with Mungrel gone. 'What about Mung … Mr Mundle, he won't know…'

Miss Tish waved her hand. 'We can catch him up. I'm sure he won't mind. Are you going on, Anna, or can I get the Tim Tams?'

Miss Tish was sent for the biscuits, the rest got comfortable, no one shone their torch into the shadows. The dream about the deb dress had struck a cord; we were keen to see what Anna would do with the epic.

As the blue girl headed for home-room she saw two year seven students, a boy and a girl, with a blue line across their faces. People had been pointing her out all day as the girl that had walked through the whole school smoking. The year sevens were awed. It was amusing, she thought, but she was a little annoyed as well—these stupid little year sevens could not begin to understand the depth of feeling that had led to an impulsive act. As she was walking out the front gate the arty crew in year ten knelt down in a row and salaamed, bowed to her; they had paper rolled as cigarettes in their mouths. They weren't blue, but it was a fair bet that they would be the next day and eventually someone would call her in and ask for an explanation. One she would be unable to give.

She had no desire to make things any more sensational then they were already, Anna continued. She didn't even have her usual smoke on the bus in case it sparked more foolishness.

She wondered if she was as foolish, so easily impressed; was she just one of the mindless teenagers brainwashed by parents, teachers and the media? What was hip or cool could change overnight. Some movie star would appear in a new hairstyle and the next day it was chill. All she had to do to become a celebrity was to do one outrageous thing; it really was easy to impress them. Was she that bad? What could she do with this new-won fame; she could start an uprising, a rebellion. No, she did not wish to be a leader. In fact, she wanted nothing more to do with this whole place.

She tried to imagine herself going to school tomorrow, but she couldn't. She sat down and tried to do some homework, but it was like it had been in class, the words refused to make sense. There seemed no point. She wandered around the house. The news was on in the lounge; it was all grief, death, destruction and balding men talking the world away.

It all seemed such a game; it made as much sense as the schoolbooks open on her desk, the indecipherable symbols on the white board. None of it had anything to do with her. None of them had anything to do with the questions that were eating at her soul. She wasn't sure what the questions were but unless they could be answered life was shit. Smoking seemed to help but she wasn't allowed to smoke in the house so she headed out into the crisp, purity of the night, out onto the street, under the stars. She sat on the brick pillar of the front fence and blew smoke rings around the stars.

She felt like she was seeing the stars for the first time—perhaps she was seeing with new eyes. They floated just out of reach, impossibly close white holes in the black fabric rather than white lights in the void. How could there be the fabric of space if it was a vacuum; how can there be nothing? Just the space between the stars made her head hurt.

The smoke rings she was blowing seemed to shrink the cosmos. She could imagine her tiny earth breathing and spinning beneath the array of stars, so tiny and unimportant, and she minuscule, insignificant.

The expectations her parents had of her seemed unimportant. What was the point of going to uni when the planet was dying? What was a career when some virus or other global disaster would probably kill her off? The idea of going to school tomorrow seemed crazy—life was so short, too short to do wasteful things like indulge others, doing what they expected.

She understood all this clearly, it all made sense. Yet the next morning she scrubbed at the blue in the shower, got dressed, made her lunch and headed off to school. As she was walking to the bus she noticed that there was something wrong with her eyes, things seemed to go out of focus. The world seemed to have faults in it like a mirror cracked, everything seemed new, or she was seeing it for the first time, it was like the stars from last night. She ignored everyone and climbed onto the bus. She was in a whirl, she felt a tremendous energy and she felt like she was going to explode. She jumped to her feet and screamed, 'STOP!' She was four seats behind the driver. So urgent was the scream that he locked up the brakes and brought the bus to a shuddering halt, skewed across the country road. The bruised and protesting kids were all looking at the blue girl who had somehow kept her feet. She did not acknowledge them or the lecture she was getting from the driver. She simply stood at the door until the driver opened it. She walked down the steps and off down the road. 'It was like,' the driver said later, 'she was listening to something that no one else could hear'.

end Anna's bit

Anna's new bit of the epic was pretty heavy; she's had to fill me in so I could write it, as I couldn't remember much of it. I'm still not sure what the hell she was talking about. I thought I'd never be able to tell stories like that. I guess she was telling adult stories. I was still thinking it cool to walk into school smoking. I also think part of me didn't want to ask those questions. I was happy to float along.

We had a good talk that night. The fact that we had been through something of an ordeal, the fact that Mungrel wasn't there, that we were pretty much alone and reliant on each other drew us closer. We were all thinking a bit more than usual. We weren't taking anything for granted any more. I realised for the first time that we are pretty insulated from the real world. We are protected so much that our world is school and TV. Out in the wild, survival was not taken for granted, comfort was not important and you realise you're never really safe.

Never really safe, I hated and liked it. I hated the fact that I was a coward and I might lose it, if tested. Why, the day before I'd been five metres from the track and I was shitting myself. What if the axe-murderer walked into the campfire light? What would I do?

I liked me better out there; I was worth more, of more value. I realised as I thought about the blue girl walking away from the school bus that I didn't like myself much back in the real world; I was a nobody, a bit of a tryhard. I felt really confused, restless but really alive. It seems strange but for a minute I wanted the camp to go on forever. I wanted to hug Becc. I wasn't being sexy; I just liked these people, liked being in the bush. I think it was then that I decided I wanted to tell part of the epic and it didn't really matter if Mungrel didn't make it back—he was already overdue. We would be okay.

We were talking about where the blue girl was going. Nearly everyone had stories about running away when they were little. When I was little I'd put two Anzac biscuits in the back of my trike and journeyed up the hill to the park. I was gunna teach them! I waited until I was starving but when I got home they hadn't even noticed I'd gone. Dicko reckoned his Mum had offered to pack his bag for him, and that didn't surprise us. We'd often suggested he piss off. But he told us by the time she'd put in all the things he'd wanted he couldn't lift the bag. Tanja suggested that if she were Dicko's mother she would have carried the bloody bag for him. Steph reckons he's a good argument for retrospective abortion. I reckon that's tight.

We also talked about friends we'd had at school and how once you get to secondary school your friends change. Some of the girls had the same friends all the way through. Dicko and Adam are both loners. Even though Dicko is smart and Adam is not too hot at school work, they hang around together. I don't think they really like each other though, they're always fighting. They don't really fit in, they just clown around, make you laugh and we accept them because we like having someone around to hang it on.

Matt is a loner too, but because he wants to be alone. Everyone likes him but he knows what he wants and he doesn't really need us. I don't think I'm a misfit or as independent as Matt. I'm not sure where I fit in with the guys, I don't really play footy with the jocks either. I play, but if I'm honest, I'm not much good at it. Girls play different games, you can talk to them, and guys don't talk much. When a guy you've grown up with takes his own life and none of his friends have a clue what he was thinking, you gotta wonder. The guys think it pretty cool to be popular with the girls—once I started hanging with the girls, I got on with the guys better. Rowan the school stud actually came to ask my advice about Teal.

We laughed about grade five when we used to go out with each other. We didn't talk to each other, or play together; you were just going out. There were a couple of games of kiss chasey until it got outlawed as too dangerous; seems kids didn't realise you should slow down before you try to kiss someone!

We didn't really talk about going out now, but were all thinking about it. Year ten was pretty busy but there was still a fair bit going on. We were looking at each other in a new light. I went to my tent to get a jacket and just happened to worm my way in next to Becc at the fire. It was really bad timing because Sarah was just paying out on men. 'All men are bastards,' she was saying. I'd learnt not to argue. Poor old Dicko took the bait and was getting monstered.

We began talking about the future and marriage and what we wanted out of life. When Becc said that she was going to get married and have four kids I nearly moved back to the other side of the fire. But then she said that wouldn't be for years, not until she had a career. Becc was leaning on my legs and I started playing with the fine, wispy hair that had escaped from her ponytail.

We talked about a kid at school that was pregnant. We all felt pretty sorry for her or thought she was crazy for keeping the kid, it was going to ruin her life. Kelly said she should have listened more in science, but Becc whispered to me that she was pissed off her head when she got pregnant.

Becc wanted me to fill up the billy so I grabbed my torch and headed down to the river. I jumped down onto the rocky beach. It was a metre below the bank on which we were camped. I noticed a wet spot on the larger stones. There were two footprints, wet footprints. I stood there looking at them for ages before I realised what was strange. None of our people were in bare feet and these were really wet feet. Someone had crossed the creek and sat there listening to us talk. They must have squatted or I think we would have seen them. I swung the torch around but he was gone—I assumed it was our friend the muddy axe-murderer, because that was exactly what he'd done the previous night.

I felt the night crawl under my jumper and run down my spine. Either he was working out who to kill first or he wanted to listen to our fire-side chat. The skin on the back of my neck went spastic and I nearly leapt back up the bank. I stood there with my guts turning over, amazed that no one noticed how green I looked. I hated these shocks. It was like having unexpected buckets of water thrown over you and the worst thing about it was you could never tell if it would be scalding hot or freezing cold. I was just pleased with myself that I didn't start blubbering.

I wasn't sure what to do about the footprints so I sat by the fire as the group talked about their favourite cartoons. I wanted to tell someone but wasn't sure if it was a good idea to frighten shit out of everyone. Becc had already noticed something so I closed my eyes against the campfire smoke and kept my head down.

Anna was busy explaining to Kelly that when we look out into space we are looking into the past; we are looking at the history of the universe. If I had been paying attention my brain would have been switching to overload. Anna went on to wonder about the fact that on the lip of a black hole gravity is infinite which creates anti-matter which could create parallel universes. Yeah! Right! At least I think that was what she was saying. I was wondering if we were going to get murdered in our beds. I was wishing Mungrel would show up; I would have told him about our visitor. It wasn't my job to protect all these people, but it was down to me. He'd put a hand on my shoulder on his way past. 'You'll be right.' He'd said. It seemed that there was no one else to tell. I could sit there and piss myself or I could do something.

I considered telling Miss Tish but I couldn't see what she would do that we couldn't do without her. I guess I didn't want to worry her. I decided that Matt was the only one I could really rely on—I wasn't sure if Dicko would insist on telling everyone. Becc said later I was being sexist. I guess I was. Sexist and stupid.

I moved over to where Matt was sitting with Kelly and waited until I had the chance to speak to him without the others hearing. I wasn't sure if I was being stupid. We knew there was someone out there but we didn't know if they were really a threat. We didn't know what had happened to Big Bill. He might have just got himself lost or maybe he'd had his tongue cut off and rammed down his throat. If this stranger in the bush had really meant us harm he'd had plenty of opportunities. The only thing we could be sure of was that this person was pretty keen to spy on us. It was pretty game to sneak up on us twice. It was clear that he was more comfortable in the night bush than we were. Given that I was feeling extremely uncomfortable, it was a sure bet that he was feeling a lot more comfortable than me. I just couldn't bring myself to break the mood of the group.

I eventually got Matt to go and take a look at the footprints on the stones. He pretty much said what I had been thinking—there wasn't much point in telling Miss Tish but it was a good idea to keep watch, just in case. We decided to take turns. We had to finish our whispered conference as a couple of the girls headed off to clean their teeth. No one had had much sleep the previous night so some were already heading for bed. Matt and I returned to the fire only to find Becc and Kelly looking at each other and then looking at us. It seemed we would have to tell at least two more people.

'I want to add something to the epic. Anna's bit was great but Mungrel said it can take any style, I was thinking about a mural, should I do it now?' Nikki was looking around. She'd been really quiet, but it could have been the fact that she carried a fair bit of weight and was probably working hard just to keep up. Her best friends were too wussy to come on camp so she was pretty much on her own. She ended up sharing with Steph. She was pretty alternative; she was the only kid with a stud in her nose and she wore full-on Gothic stuff.

'This will be a bit different and I'm not sure how it might fit in, it... might be something completely different.'

People looked pretty relieved to have some more epic distraction, no one was used to going to bed at eight-thirty and there's not much else to do once you've finished staring at the stars— even if they were glorious that night; we'd already seen a couple of shooting stars. The cool change hadn't lasted so it was cool but clear. Those that had been heading for bed settled in, unwilling to miss the next episode. As Nikki began her part of the story in her thin voice, I wondered if our barefoot friend was out there listening. I listened to Nikki but I also listened to the sound of the trees, the river and the night listening to us. I really enjoyed her story, and I seem to remember it pretty well, despite the fact that I was on the edge of panic.

Nikki's bit

Not far from here, in the Lerderderg Gorge, there is a clearing bathed in sunlight. There is the sound of scraping, metal on stone, and bird song. Adam's enigmatic character from the Nullarbor is following a walking track that meets a number of others like it at this clearing.

He is following no map; he comes to a fork in the track and knows which way to go. He finally emerges into the clearing and drops his swag by the dying fire, from which a thin line of smoke divides the sky. There is a tarpaulin slung amongst the trees and evidence of someone camping here. The pile of ash suggests that there have been many fires here over time.

He is a day's walk from any major road but he is under the flight path of Melbourne's international airport. He looks up at the distant rumble, but the plane is too high and has already vanished from the portion of sky he can see through the trees.

He follows the scraping sound towards a huge sandstone wall and stands twenty metres away and watches someone lean and brown wearing only shorts and singlet perched on a ledge fifteen metres off the ground.

The walker assumes the figure on the cliff has a hammer and chisel that he or she uses, sometimes to tap and then scrape at the rock. From this distance you can make out the vague patterns in the stone. Further across the face of the cliff you can see a much deeper shape, carved in relief. It looks like a tiny figure, beautifully detailed, against a great empty slope. But the figure is not tiny; given his distance from it he judges the figure must be at least life-sized. Our wanderer with the blue tattoo on his forehead walks back to the fire, feeds it and puts the billy on to boil.

The sun tints everything orange as it prepares to leave the bush. The walker looks up from the fire to see

*a lean, nut-brown woman covered in stone dust
dump her tools and put on a jumper. The walker lifts
the billy out of the coals as the woman holds out her
battered mug. There is no greeting, nor is there any
apparent surprise that the walker has arrived; there is
a sense of ease, comfort. They sit sipping their tea.
They have not exchanged a word but you get the feeling that their knowledge of each other reaches back
beyond memory.*

*The blue girl has stood there blinking for some
minutes before the walker takes his own cup and
hands it to her. His lips do not move but his eyes say,
What kept you? We have been waiting. She follows him
to the fire and slides into the dust. She has been walking since pink dawn and it is now deep blue night. She
looks at the silent strangers and feels she knows them,
has always known them like some uncle and aunt who
were around a lot when you were small but who you
haven't seen for years. She gulps the lukewarm tea,
looks at the sky and thinks, I have seen that colour
somewhere before, puts her head on her blue arm and
slides into sleep.*

'This is the same blue girl?' I had to know. I
was amazed that the epic had leapt from the
school bus and a Mack truck into this strange
gathering. Nikki nodded that it was the same girl.
'What about the mural you said you had?'

Nikki looked at me patiently.

'You want me to finish?'

As usual I felt a fool. Dicko was sitting beside me, so I didn't even have to get up. I was a little anxious trying to keep up with the story and listen to the bush. I had been really keen to tell part of the epic and I thought that I could have, when the story was realistic. Now I thought it was getting out of my reach. I couldn't make up stories like Nikki's. I'm not sure what it all meant but I really liked it, if that makes sense.

It amazed me that people could imagine things so differently. Mungrel had started off with this grungy, dope smoking, teen burnout party, then Anna and Matt continued with slightly more realistic or everyday stories. Then we had Adam's truckie out of the blue and now Nikki had turned the whole thing into a mystical, symbolic thing. It was time to shut up; everyone was looking at Nikki, waiting for the next part of the story. You got the feeling at school that Nikki got pretty sick of us. We weren't all that comfortable with her, or she, I guess, with us. But she had centre stage now and people were quite happy to listen. I wondered if her whole story would be silent, no one in it had said a word yet. A bit like Nikki at school. Apart from class, where she had to talk, I couldn't remember Nikki talking at all. But now, out in the bush, Nikki was really talking.

The blue girl wakes to find herself wrapped in a blanket, stiff and still exhausted. She feels like she has not moved in the night. She looks around the campsite; the party, smoking at school, getting off the bus, walking into the bush, all seems like years ago.

She can hear a scraping noise; she follows the noise and arrives at the sandstone wall. On a ledge high above the valley floor the woman is perched. She is busy sculpting shapes from the stone. There is a steady shower of sand and chips. The blue girl realises that the whole wall is covered by designs, mostly low enough to reach from the ground but some up higher, some she can make out forty metres above the ground. No two are similar. Most are simple shapes, like the hallmarks you find on the bottom of pottery or jewellery. Other shapes are more complex—curious animals, geometric shapes like runes, some like brands. There are some the size of paintings and a couple of murals that run for metres. The more complex ones have colour; some have natural ochres, dusty reds and golds, others have washed-out colour or what looks like lime wash and charcoal.

She steps back from the wall to get a good look at the largest figure, high on the central face. It is a relief carving of a human figure, life sized. It would have taken months to carve this shape from the surrounding stone—even from this distance the girl can make out the folds of the clothes. The stone figure has its back to the viewer and is walking up a road. The actual road has been carved from around the figure, and the perspective lines make it look like the figure is walking up the hill and would eventually disappear up the natural chimney. The crest of the hill is decorated with a fence and trees to represent the skyline. The scale and illusion created by this are stunning. The girl is wondering at the reason for such a detailed work in such an isolated place and why sculpt a figure that is walking away from the viewer, when the man appears.

He is leaning against the bole of an ancient gum, staring at the wall, just above her head. He motions her to look at the wall. There just above eye level is an exquisite lizard or more correctly a gecko, sapphire blue and missing a right front leg, so that as it coils in upon itself it forms a circle.

She has seen the lizard before. Then it strikes her. She looks back at the man smiling at her, and there on his forehead is the blue tattoo of the lizard. She has no choice but to smile back. It seems each of these symbols belongs to some individual—is something private and significant. She opens her mouth to ask but he raises a finger, silencing her. There will be no questions.

There was a murmur from the group when they recognised the tattoo. Nikki was not quite done.

The couple feed her and allow her to follow them around the natural amphitheatre, but they do not speak and otherwise ignore her. The woman eventually beckons her up to the ledge where she has been working. She carefully scales the ledges and precarious gaps to arrive panting and somewhat spooked at the woman's side. She is lovingly shown the latest scar on the rock. Deeply etched into the sandstone is a little girl, the type of figure a child might draw, the dress a simple triangle. The face is childishly innocent with wide, bewildered eyes and, over the mouth, a tight gag, silencing the figure. The woman runs her fingers over the gagged mouth, touches her own dry lips. Then turning to face the startled girl she touches her lips with those same dusty fingertips. Is it a blessing or is she being bound by the silence that both these severe strangers carry? As she carefully climbs down from the ledge, she feels changed. She shakes a little at the thought that she is no longer the same girl that marched off to school a day ago.

It takes her another day to realise what else she has to do. She finds herself a square of empty wall plus the tools and colours that the woman has left in a plastic bag at the foot of the cliff. She begins to make her mark, leave her calling card, carve her symbol into the living stone. She doesn't have to think about it for too long, nor is there any doubt about the only colour to be used. When she returns from the wall, hands shaky with the fatigue of carving stone, both the man and the woman have gone. The tarpaulin has been rolled up and the fire is cold. The girl looks back at the wall, wondering how many others have taken leave of this place, taking the silence and one of the many walking tracks that lead them back to the real world.

'And that's it,' Nikki informed us.

end Nikki's bit

People shook, stretched, murmured approval, some actually applauded. I had forgotten about our uninvited visitor. I was trying to work out what symbol I would have put on the wall.

'What was the symbol?' Miss Tish wanted to know.

'Not telling,' smiled Nik. 'I know my symbol, but someone might need to create their own version, depending on where they take the story.'

'That was shit-hot, Nik!' Matt claimed. 'You've given me an idea but I'll have to think about it some more.'

No one wanted to really discuss what the epic was revealing. We were sure now that there was an amazing person inside that fat body. Somehow at school you never get the opportunity for these things to come out. The strange yella fella in the bush, this scary freak had changed the group, maybe changed us.

I wanted to ask Nik who the people at the clearing were, but I'd never spoken to her, not since we gave her shit in gym. She never did anything; she was always sick or not changed. I wondered for the first time if that was our fault. It must have been the guilt, but it was then that I remembered that I was going to keep an eye out for the axe-murderer. Listening to Nik's story I had forgotten. I was amazed I could be that scared one minute and forget the next.

The rest of the group was talking about tattoos. Dicko was going to get a gargoyle on his arm when he was old enough. He was always drawing satanic stuff on his books. One of the teachers went ape shit when they saw a swastika on one of his books. He couldn't understand the lecture he got about evil. The teacher couldn't understand why he didn't understand. The girls were talking about getting something tasteful like a butterfly tatt on their butt but they were concerned that it would hurt. That was Tanja, who has a belly ring, which I suppose is what you call an earring in the belly button.

Matt was giving me the eye; I followed him towards the river. 'Nik's story, cool yeah? But we'd better take a look around.' We jumped down from the bank onto the river stones.

By the time I'd regained my balance Matt had his torch on and was staring at the new, wet footprints. Then we were both playing the beam of our torches madly around us. My skin crawled as another bucket of cold water hit me. The visitor had been back, crouching only metres from the fire, listening. He could come and go as he pleased. He must have been so quick that as soon as someone stood up and walked towards the river he could disappear. We could feel his eyes upon us. He must have been able to see us but we couldn't see him. He probably wasn't even using a torch so he couldn't see the evidence he left on the river stones. 'What I don't get is, why is he listening?' whispered Matt.

It was then Becc and Kelly appeared on the bank above us.

'He's back, isn't he?' demanded Becc.

Matt woke me at two as we'd agreed; he was freezing and headed straight off to bed. Becc and

Kelly were going to do the last shift together. I could hardly keep my eyes open so I hopped over to the fire, still in my bag. I took my arms out of the bag so I could grab the stick we had by the fire. Even with the extra wood I put on the fire I was freezing, so I put my arms back in the bag and zipped it up.

Then I sat and imagined. I imagined that the axe-murderer was crouching just below the bank. I imagined I could hear him breathe above the sound of the river. I imagined he was all around, sneaking up. I imagined I was falling asleep, then the fire cracked and the adrenalin rush felt like more ice water. I couldn't imagine feeling so shit-scared and so sleepy at the same time, then I imagined my eyes were closing all by themselves and I was falling asleep—and I was.

My greatest fear was that I would fall asleep, which I did. The next most feared thing was that the axe-murderer would be able to creep into the camp without my knowing. He had shown that he was far better in the bush than we were. The amazing thing then was that when I woke I was standing. Somehow I had leapt clean out of my sleeping bag and I was holding the stout stick that I had selected as my weapon. I should have realised that something was wrong. That sneaky axe-murderer had already crept up on us at least three times. This time I could hear him coming through the bush. I should have realised, but you don't think too clearly when you've been woken by an axe-murderer.

I raced over to Matt. He groaned when I shook him, then he leapt up like he'd been stung. I knew my mind was working slowly but Matt came alive from a standing start. He was out of the tent, had located the source of the sound, had his stick ready and was moving towards the edge of the camp where he thought the noise was coming from.

I remember thinking he was headed in the wrong direction when he stood on Steph and Sarah's tent peg in his bare feet. The peg came out of the ground, down came the tent. He staggered through the guy ropes on Miss Tish's tent and was resolutely marching towards where he thought the attack was coming from. He was limping but determined not to let the protests starting up from Steph distract him.

Her noise was covering all the other sounds. Matt was hissing at Steph to shut up. She just thought it was some stupid prank, and was telling the night that whoever had pulled out her peg better put it back before she came out and shoved it up their arse. Next, Miss Tish emerges from her tent. Matt, the girls and I had agreed not to use torches because they made us too easy a target. It gave someone without a torch a real advantage. It was fairly cloudy but we could see quite well until Miss Tish turns on her shit-hot, halogen-head torch. First she looks at me. I feel this pain rip open the back of my brain and the night gets real dark. Then she looks at Matt and blinds him. One minute we feel pretty under control—we can see in the dark, we can hear the enemy. Now we hear nothing but Steph bitchin' at the top her voice and see nothing but burn marks on our retina.

We ran around for a few minutes trying to get Steph to quiet down, and Miss Tish to turn the flamethrower off. We explain in our panic that there is someone out there. Half the camp is awake now, all asking what is happening only to be hissed at. Then Matt hisses at me to come, he can hear him again. As we listen I'm sure it sounds like two people. The sound is coming closer; we get ready, crouching by the base of a big gum. I'm suddenly thirsty and I need a piss. I can just see Matt in the gloom—my night sight is slowly coming back but not fast enough. He looks ready to cry. I grip the stick and realise as I wait that I'm on the right of the track and I'm right-handed. I'm hopeless with my left hand; it has no power.

I'm sure that if I don't nail this guy the first time I will be incapable of fighting him. I will freeze and he will kill us all. I decide to take a step back and lift the stick above my head so I can bring it straight down on this guy's head. It catches on a branch in the darkness above my head, I panic and heave downward to free it. It comes clear suddenly. It's headed for Matt's head. I try to pull up but am too slow. Matt gets a glancing blow on the shoulder and falls sideways in his efforts to avoid being brained. I overbalance so that Matt recovers first. Out the corner of my eye I see him swing his stick—I think at first it is at me but it is over my head. The axe-murderer is behind me. Miss Tish yells, in panic I assume. I swing round with my stick. I'm on my right hand now and hoping Matt's follow-through has got him out of the way. I plant my feet, bend my back and swing at where the axe-murderer's head should be.

I gave it everything I had.

With the noise we had been making Mungrel was expecting something so as Matt swung he was able to get his hands up in time. He was just bowled over as he tried to get out of the way.

Adam was right behind him. He didn't see anything, he said, 'until va truck 'it me in va mouf'.

By first light Mungrel had put as many of Adam's teeth as he could find into a carton of long-life milk, stopped most of the bleeding and was getting ready to take Adam back up the hill. He tried putting the teeth back in, but Adam's lips were a mess. He needed a dental surgeon; Mungrel had tied up his jaw because he thought the jaw might be broken. Just as well Adam couldn't talk because he would have called us the biggest pack of friggin idiots ever to draw breath. I must admit I agreed with him. I never felt such a dickhead. Even if it was an accident, we really stuffed up and now Mungrel had to leave us to look after ourselves again. He looked really stuffed—so did Adam. That made me twice as guilty. At least we found out what happened to Mr Tuwhati.

Mungrel told us that Big Bill was safe. It seems he'd lost sight of the axe-murderer after following him for some time and then was a bit lost so he headed to where he knew the four-wheel drive track was. The axe-murderer had been heading away from the camp so Big Bill figured we were safe at least. He expected to meet up with Mr

Cream in the backup four-wheel drive at the top of the track and ring the group to let them know what was going on. Meanwhile, Mr Cream had been bitten by jumping ants and had to take himself into hospital to get some anti-histamines, so there was no one at the top of the track. Big Bill had had to walk about eighteen kilometres to Blackwood in the dark before he found a phone. He got Mr Cream on the mobile, only to find Mr Cream was back at the top of the track. What a total balls-up!

Mr Cream was under doctor's orders to go home so Big Bill drove him. He, Mr Cream that is, had pain all up his right arm, sweats and twitching. So what's new, I wanted to ask when I heard. Big Bill then came looking for us to let us know what was going on. Mungrel said he was stuffed. He met Mungrel and Adam coming up Whisky Track, which was handy because it seemed the mobile phones just weren't working in the gorge.

They had agreed that the bloke in the bush didn't seem to be too much of a worry since he had headed in the other direction when Big Bill was following him. They would have been worried if they had seen the tracks by the river that Matt and I had been looking at about the same time they were having their discussion.

Big Bill agreed to stay with the four-wheel drive and head in from Mt Blackwood so we could get Marjorie out without climbing straight up the side of the gorge. It meant that we had to go further downstream and then take the best part of a day to walk the group up Ah Kow Track. So we would still have two days to walk, but if we took it gently Marjorie might be able to walk out by herself. Big Bill would walk in down Ah Kow Track to meet us and help carry Marjorie if needed. The walk would be a little shorter than originally planned, we would pop out a few Ks earlier and we could ring the bus company to change the pick up.

I stuffed all that up with my big stick.

It was first light when we got all this information from Mungrel. He'd collected Adam's teeth and was getting ready to head back up the Razorback Track. Because I had smashed Adam's face in, their nice plans were totally stuffed. Mungrel would have to try and ring Big Bill from the top of the track. They would have to try and get Adam to hospital and then both meet us that night at Ah Kow's Ruin and then walk us out from there the next day. The only trouble was Miss Tish would have to take us downstream by herself. We'd told everyone about the footprints.

We had to. I had to justify trying to kill a teacher and actually smashing in the face of another student. I'd never heard Adam so quiet. I never thought I'd say it but I just wanted him to say something dumb. I didn't really hear his voice again until we all got back to school.

Mungrel had this big debate with Miss Tish. He originally wanted to send her up the Razorback with Adam so he could stay with the group.

Tish was worried that she might get lost trying to find her way out. She said she would be better off with the group following the river—there was no way she could get lost and Ah Kow's Ruin, where they would have to camp, was really easy to spot. She also pointed out that Adam looked really stuffed from their forced march up the Razorback and might collapse, not to mention the fact that I had assaulted him in the face with half a gum tree.

He was really pale, had lost a fair bit of blood and was clearly in some sort of shock. Tish was concerned that if he collapsed on the way up she wouldn't be able carry him. Being unfamiliar with the area she wasn't confident about going for help or relying on the dodgy phones. She was clearly happier about staying with the group and coping with our night visitor, who hadn't done any harm so far, except frighten us to death. I've got to say I was impressed. She was pretty gutsy and had stayed pretty calm, even when Matt and I had gone ape with our clubs.

I'm not sure if Mungrel really believed us about the footprints and trusted Big Bill's story about the axe-dude heading away from us. I felt like I'd let him down. I think he just wanted to crawl into a tent and go to sleep and I felt a bit guilty. At this stage I would have wanted to slip into a sleeping bag. He'd sat up and watched for the axe-murderer most of the first night, had done a full day's walk, done another day's walk up the Razorback, turned around and walked back again in the dark and spent the rest of the night tending to a kid with a smashed face. Now he was about to head up the Razorback yet again. Mungrel always looked pretty fit and young. Someone had told me he was nearly fifty. For the first time I realised he was older than my Dad. Dad thought walking to the fridge a big deal.

I remember being really sick of the whole thing, the camp, the fear, my own stuff ups. I was also exhausted, past tired. The fear was eating away at my energy and our situation wasn't getting any better. I watched Mungrel and Adam head out of camp as the sun came over the lip of the gorge and to tell the truth I wished I were going with them. It was then Miss Tish came over and told me to get a couple of hours' sleep.

I was lying in my tent, smelling my own stale sweat; it sounded like everyone else was already asleep and I wondered about the guy out there in the bush. I had the whole group around me, one more sleep and I would be back in my own soft bed. Who would choose to live out here? I kept thinking about the axe-dude sitting silent in the bush listening to strangers, and the silent people in the epic, not talking. It was then that I decided to tell the next part of the story. I went to sleep working out that when the blue girl carved her symbol in the stone she was choosing silence. She might return to her life but she wouldn't speak again.

dreamy days, green hornet nights

I thought it was a dream! Becc was stroking my hair, kissing me lightly on the eyes and then my nose and then teasing my lips with light feathery kisses, then the sound of laughter round the campfire. It was real, I was awake.

'Miss Tish said we gotta get going, I just thought I'd give you a wake up call,' Becc whispered. She gave the pup tent in my sleeping bag a friendly pat, smiled and crawled out of the tent. I groaned.

'Are you all right in there?' It was Miss Tish. I told her I was fine and wondered if she had seen Becc come out of my tent. 'We need to get going so we can get to camp before dark, okay?'

I told her, 'Fine, I'll start packing.'

Becc had smelt so good and clean. I ached for her to come back but at least she had banished the feelings of last night. She probably knew how bad I was feeling about Adam and decided to help me out. Some help, she'd given me such a hard time it was ten minutes before I could leave the tent without people thinking I had a gun in my pocket.

We were pretty late getting started after everyone had a sleep. The girls were having a lunchtime swim even though it was freezing. Most of them had T-shirts on but it was easy to tell how cold the water was. I tried to get the image of pink puppy-dog noses out of my mind and kept myself busy packing up the tent that was supposed to have been for Adam and Mr Mundle. I think I was still in a dream as we walked that morning.

We were having a late lunch by the river when I tried to tell them the part of the epic I had been thinking about since packing up the tent. Ah Kow's Ruin wasn't far downstream but Miss Tish was keen to let us take a break and a swim every so often to make sure Marjorie would make the distance. We were all a little stuffed so we hadn't talked much and I think we were all a little conscious about being watched so I think people were keen to have someone tell them a story.

'Next part of the epic about to begin,' I announced. People started to get comfortable and were looking at me when Miss Tish pushed in.

'Can I back track a bit, I'd like to write a new letter. It is in the mailbox when the blue girl arrives home from the bush,' Miss Tish was looking for approval.

'I really liked the letter, I thought it was really sad,' Anna protested.

'Why do you want to change it now?' Becc had liked it too, it seemed. 'I thought it sounded like they had something special, I liked it a lot, Miss.'

'I'm not rewriting, I'm doing the next letter. It's from the same bloke but a week or so later.'

Dicko was into pushing his luck. 'You know that first letter about the girl getting dropped. How much of that was true?' Dicko promptly groaned and sank to the ground to reveal Fei. She was four foot nothing tall but she was angry.

'You do not ask rude questions.' Fei had arrived at school only weeks after she arrived in the country; she didn't say much but had mastered the language in six months. It was easy to forget she was around, she was so quiet and studious, but sometimes she gave us guys looks that could kill. You got the sense that she appreciated what we had a lot more than we did. I'd never seen her hit anyone before. Dicko was rubbing his kidneys as he picked himself up; he was watching Fei very carefully.

'I'll admit it was partly autobiographical, but only part,' admitted Miss Tish, 'and I'm not telling which part. Anyway, there is this new letter in the mailbox when she gets back. Don't we have to give her a name? No?'

Tish's bit

Dear whoever!

I saw you sitting in the bus on your way to school and I was really frightened. It was the look on your face. Remember the talk we had in the mullock heaps out back of Lauriston about suicide and stuff. Remember I said you had to look death in the face—well that was bullshit. Respect death but give him a wide berth, don't give him the time of day!

I think you'd know Mark Sievers, you would have met him at parties, he was at the Rubber Chicken Gig—well, they found him hanging from a hay shed. No reason, I reckon he was just confused; he wasn't thinking clearly enough when he weighed up life or death.

You should have seen his folks. If he'd any idea about how shattered they would be, he wouldn't have even thought about it. I'm really clear now, he was really stupid, suicide is just plain stupid and I'm really frightened that some idiot will think it cool and copy him. I'll be really angry if that happens.

When I saw the look on your face I knew the dark side was winning. I know I rejected your love but I haven't rejected you. I wasn't strong enough to be in love with you but let me help you. Contact me, I'm not going to any more funerals. The worst that life has to offer is better than the alternative.

Call me!

Love, the Bastard.

P.S. why was your face blue????????????

end Tish's bit

Miss Tish looked up to see Tanja, Fei and Nancy giving Dicko a hard time. It seems he'd been annoying them with a grass stalk while Miss Tish was telling her letter.

'Time to get going,' she said. For the first time the audience was restless. I thought at first it was because nothing happens in a letter. As I started walking I realised it was probably the suicide stuff. Mark was a real person; Miss Tish had brought the real world into the epic. No one wanted to talk about Mark, we all knew him, but we couldn't understand why he'd killed himself. It had made everyone depressed for weeks; we were walking around being really careful with each other. Nathan started making suicide jokes. 'What's green and hangs from trees?' he'd say. 'Unripe bananas,' he'd answer and go off pissing himself because we'd be thinking about Mark.

Miss Tish was scanning our faces, 'I'm sorry. I didn't want to make it too depressing but I was worried about her attitude—there was too little hope, things were too bleak. I just wanted to make sure the epic kept going until Mr Mundle can catch up, he'd really like to hear his little trial epic.'

'Little try, gone ballistic,' laughed Tanja.

'The only rule is that you don't kill off the story!' chanted Anna.

'Does that mean you can change the direction if it suits you?' It was Matt asking; he had been frowning since the letter. He seemed to resent it. I couldn't see his problem, although he had been mates with Mark. Maybe he knew more stuff than the rest of us. We'd never talked about it.

Miss Tish looked at Matt. 'If someone else wants to deal with suicide, Matt, my little letter isn't going to stop them.'

Matt looked Tish in the eyes. 'No happy endings, please.'

Miss Tish returned Matt's stare. Matt turned his back and picked up his pack. Everyone else grabbed theirs.

Matt appeared to make a decision and walked back into the centre of the group. He looked funny, because his pack was nearly as big as he was, but his eyes were blazing.

Matt's bit

'Here is the next bit of the epic!' he announced.

The blue girl steps down from the bus. She has just made her way back from the bush. She hasn't got home yet, she hasn't looked in the letterbox, she walks past the front of the bus out onto the road. She is hit by a '68 Volkswagen Punch Buggy, spins high into the air and hits, head first with a sound like a smashed melon, grey matter leaks from her ears, her eyes and her nose. The bus driver stands distracted. He is listening. He hears, high up in the air, a solitary voice laughing, a laugh that echoes through all time. The End!

end Matt's bit

Matt turned on his heel, the epic was stuffed; he had broken the only rule. We looked at each other and followed Matt downstream. I thought I could hear him laughing and I didn't like it. I guess I felt he had killed something more than the epic.

I guess I was pissed off with Matt, because I had the next bit worked out. I was pissed off because he killed the story; he was upset with Tish for wanting to keep the character alive. Because a teacher says not to do something you go ahead and do it—real mature. The epic had become important to the group, it had kept us calm and together, and Matt had thrown that away. It belonged to us all, he had no right. All of a sudden we were all pissed off at each other, pissed off at the camp, pissed off at ourselves, pissed off at the axe-murderer. It was broad daylight and I was as scared as I had been for the whole camp; we were vulnerable because we were alone; we were alone so we were dangerous. All because Matt killed off a piece of fiction. I'd never thought of what we do to each other as violent but it is, much worse than physical violence in some ways. As I walked along I wished Tish had never brought up the suicide stuff.

I decided not to think about it. Instead I began to really see what I was passing through. I realised that the track we were following had been an aqueduct. There were stone foundations and walls everywhere so that the channel could stay level. They must have moved tons of stone. My idea of wilderness changed.

I also noticed that the country changed dramatically every time we went around a bend. Where the sun could reach the banks of the river the vegetation was dry, harsh and prickly, the soil flinty. The permanently shaded bends were covered in damp rot, ferns, and grey-green lichens. The more sand about, the more wombat shit. It's great how they like doing it on raised areas. I found out since that it's because their back is so rigid and their poo so dry they have to snap it off. I wanted to meet one. Their poo is cuboid. That means they have a square arsehole. I call Mr Morris Wombat now because he is a square arsehole.

The more fertile the soil, the bigger the tree— then I was thinking about suicide again. The bigger trees only grow on the shaded damp sides but the soil is still rocky. A lot of the bigger trees just fall out of the soil. If the tree can't get down enough of a root system it falls over. Maybe that's what happens to teens who suicide. It's not the strong winds of stress that knock them over; it's just that they aren't rooted strongly enough. The soil is too rocky. Becc was only a couple of metres ahead of me. Girls don't kill themselves as much.

There was a gust that sounded like a tumult in the treetops. Maybe girls bend in the gale better; you need strong foundations to sway. Young tall trees that reach above the shelter of the gorge for the first time are the most vulnerable to the wind.

If I had any brains I'd give a copy of this to my English teacher and my biol teacher. Maybe not; I've got Mr Morris for biol this semester.

We walked in silence most of the afternoon. Everyone seemed to be quite happy to stay with his or her own thoughts. The track beside the river was pretty overgrown and it made it hard to walk beside each other. The other thing was the bush, the gorge was really steep so not too much light got in. It was the closest to real rain forest that we had seen; there were ferns and moss, everything seemed to be damp. It seemed more untouched; I felt that we all got quieter. It could have been Matt's brat attack but I think it was also the bush.

Part of me was thinking that I'd be home next day, but part of me really enjoyed the walking. My feet weren't hurting, my pack seemed lighter with most of the food gone, my legs seemed stronger; I just felt more at home. If not for a certain yella axe-murderer I could understand spending a lot of time out there and really enjoying it. I really enjoyed the idea that I had my whole world on my back. My house, my kitchen, my bed, my wardrobe, I could go anywhere. I imagined being out there alone, no little brother, no TV. I liked the simple routine of cooking, packing, moving on; I only wanted more time to stop and look at the spots we just tramped through. I wanted to watch the cockies and parrots, watch the light leave the gorge. I guess I was envious of the axe-murderer.

I wasn't the only one. I caught up with Becc on one curve where we climbed away from the river. I thought at first she was taking a breather, but once I drew level I realised she was looking downstream at the river. It was going to be another cold night. It had been pretty clear all day but most of us were wearing windcheaters. The mist was starting to curl across the river, the afternoon light was angled across our line of sight and the deep green shadows of the bush looked spectacular.

'Very picturskew,' I breathed in her ear.

'It's great,' she enthused.

'Not the river, you,' I ventured. 'The view ain't bad either.' Cheesy, I know, but I had been thinking about her visits to my tent. I knew the first night had been fear. I thought she was going to think I was a dickhead after smashing Adam's face but this morning's visit was magic. I could feel the kisses on my face, and I noticed as I looked at her in profile that she had a beautiful mouth. It looked just the way it had felt when she kissed me awake—full, velvety, dreamy.

She was something else. I was thinking about the year-twelve blonde I usually thought of as sexy, but looking at Becc I wondered why I'd never really noticed her. The blonde is really skinny and wears too much make-up. Becc has great curves; she looked really cool with the backpack on and her hair tied back—like she could walk forever. She had copped a bit much sun on the cheeks but her neck was like cold white stone. I just wanted, I just had this urge to touch her skin. I had the scary thought that this might be what happened when you fell in love.

Serious freak-out warning bells! I think the strain was starting to tell, but that was what I thought. They say 'Falling in Love' and that's spot on because I felt like I was falling off a cliff, almost like I was toppling off one of the cliffs towards the river. You know you're falling and it is real scary but at the same time you don't do anything to stop it—strange stuff.

When we watched Romeo and Juliet last year I thought Romeo was a prissy wanker, but now I felt like a lovesick cow. I could see myself in pink tights chasing Becc through the Australian bush, serious freak-out. The worst part of this falling stuff was fear. I'd thought I'd been scared the last few nights, now I was petrified.

I guess both were the fear of the unknown, but the yella fella was knowable; he was either an axe-murderer or something and he would either attack or he would not. With Becc it was the unknown but it was also unknowable. I didn't know her and I didn't know me and I might never. The real difference, I guess, was that even though I was the biggest yellow-bellied coward I was choosing to be scared. I wanted this fear even though I expected it to hurt. I'd rather be beaten up bad than have Becc tell me to piss off.

What if Becc wasn't in love, what if she was just playing games and how was I going to find out without her knowing I had gone sick over her? It was one strange feeling. I'd been mesmerised; I was staring at a poisonous snake so beautiful and deadly at the same time, I just couldn't move to save myself. Becc did me a favour though. I was never as scared of the axe-murderer again. Getting stalked by an axe-murderer isn't as scary as falling in love.

As we walked on I couldn't get the idea out of my head and I just wanted to keep looking at her.

She had her hair tied back but there were these wisps of curl around her forehead. We stuck together the rest of the afternoon. We didn't talk much; she just pointed things out to me—rosellas, strange mushrooms—and I just nodded like an idiot. We had been at the same school for nearly two years but it felt like we had just met.

As I walked along behind Becc I was considering what Matt had done and wondered if Mungrel had been here, would Matt have still killed off the story? The story belonged to us all and although we were free to do what we wanted with it we had a responsibility to the group.

I thought I should bring the story back to life. I could just backtrack to Matt's death scene and then wake her up from a dream so she doesn't really get killed. Or I could've done a Stephen King—shove the brains back in and resurrect the blue girl—but somehow it didn't seem right to ignore Matt's episode. If I could just find a way to turn the epic to deal with the death, if the death of the epic could be … then I caught a glimpse of Becc.

I grabbed the back of Becc's pack so that she staggered and spun around, then I kissed her and man did she kiss me back. Even with our packs on she welded herself against me and blew my mind. By the time we came up for breath the rest of the group were out of sight around the bend. We broke into a ragged run and rounded the corner to find the whole group had stopped and were waiting for us. Becc stopped dead, I cannoned into her, everyone was watching. We were embarrassed but I don't think either of us cared too much. I was listening to the blood pounding in my ears.

Miss Tish told us to keep up, just in case, then headed off again. I grabbed the back of Becc's pack just as she was about to join the line, I couldn't resist one more blast, we were both so wired, we kept at it all the rest of the way. We were just more careful to keep up. Keeping up and being careful not to get caught meant that all the kisses were fleeting, teasing, electric. If that was bush walking I could walk a bloody long way.

We expected Mungrel and Big Bill to be at Ah Kow's ruin but when we got to the ruin there was no one there. It wasn't a surprise really; they had to get an exhausted Adam out of the gorge, get him to hospital at Bacchus Marsh, get his parents out to take over, drive back to Mt Blackwood and then walk in six kilometres to the ruin.

We felt a bit safer knowing we were only a few hours' walk from the road; we didn't feel so isolated. We figured both teachers would be stuffed so they might be taking their time, even having a sleep and just aiming to get to the ruin by nightfall. Neither of them had really slept since the camp began. Knowing the teachers would be back in camp for the night I had really relaxed about our axe-murderer; it would be somebody else's problem.

I had other plans. This was our last night, tomorrow we would be home. I might never get this chance again. The bush, Becc and, as it turned out, an inconstant moon.

It was too cold to swim when we reached Ah Kow's, but it was the best campsite yet. There was a nice grassy clearing right above a sensational swimming hole. Ah Kow must have been some determined dude because you could see where he had changed the course of the river by digging a trench that diverted the course of the river and built a race so he could wash his diggings from the mine. He must have moved a small mountain of stone with his own hands. I guess there might have been more people than just him alone. It would have been a lonely life. The hill behind the clearing was riddled with mineshafts. The isolation got me thinking about our axe-murderer again. How would you cope, what would drive someone out here? This time I found myself hoping that he might still be around, I thought we might be company for him. I guess I hadn't quite accepted that he was harmless, but he was a lonely shadow following us through the gorge. Maybe he just wanted to know how the epic turned out. Well, Matt stuffed that; he killed off the main character with a '68 VW.

The group had taken to cooking together. We'd light one big fire and some would cook on that while most of us would use our metho stoves. The tents were up, including one for Mungrel and Big Bill. People were nearly finished dinner; Dicko had been living on Coco Pops and raw two-minute noodles for the last two days, and was slinking about like a dingo waiting for any food others didn't want. Most people were on the dehydrated foods by now so there was stuff all. Then Miss Tish pulled out a packet of Tim Tams and left them sitting on a log. Dicko started to howl and froth at the mouth.

We'd had Tim Tams that first night when we'd just settled into the epic and we had our yella visitor. The truth of the matter was that we hadn't actually seen him since then, yet the fact that we thought he was out there had dominated our week—the thought of him and the story that started with a girl at a party and had ended with a '68 VW. Now there was a love story as well, and I thought, someone should write all this stuff down because no one is going to believe it.

'It's the Tim Tams, the axe-murderer only comes when you get out the Tim Tams,' declared Anna.

'We should leave them out in the bush as sacrifice to spirits,' Fei suggested. The group laughed but Fei looked serious.

'Stuff that!' Tish declared. We all laughed. 'I'm going to eat them.' Tish ripped off the wrapper and was mobbed.

My brain felt like it was going 100 Ks an hour. I had plans to spend some time with Becc but I had an epic to salvage first. As the billies boiled I cranked up my part of the epic. It was my turn.

my bit

Somewhere in outback New South Wales, there is a silent walker—a man who does not speak. In the shadow of his hat his eyes squint out at the shimmering distance. On his forehead he bears a blue tattoo of a three-legged gecko. He walks determinedly like he has an appointment, though who or what he is likely to meet out there in the emptiness is a mystery, unless it is a dreaming or a story. He suddenly reels backwards like he has been hit by a brick. Beneath his raised arm he squints at the sky. He sees it swirling, blood-red and purple. He is shocked. Someone watching would see only a befuddled man in a desert. The man with the tattoo sees a vision, a vision so clear, so important, that without hesitation he turns on his heel and walks back the way he has come.

The man with the tatt is not the only one. There is a tough-looking woman in the Flinders Rangers who nearly falls from her perch among the rocks when the vision hits. She climbs down, gathers her tools and starts walking east. Right across the country, people that the locals hardly know because they never speak, get up and leave, just walk away; from Benger, Western Australia, from Marble Bar in the north, from Rigden, Queensland—even an autistic nine-year-old from Winchelsea climbs the back fence and starts walking. He will never reach the gathering, he will be found and taken home, but the other eleven eventually arrive at the clearing where they will visit their own symbol, then gather at the foot of the rock and wait.

Some have been walking for days, but when they arrive there is no greeting; everyone is met with *silence. They wait in silence, they watch the changing sky, they eat in silence, they sleep in the dust. When the eleventh member arrives he begins to crush red dirt to powder; the rest collect yellow clay, white lime, charcoal and begin a sand drawing which contains an ancient story.*

There are places for twelve symbols in the story but there are only eleven. There is a gap in the pattern; their bodies tell that they are shattered; they sit and stare at the painting.

The man with the tattoo on his forehead leads the rest to the wall and shows them a blue Volkswagen, carved into the rock, the next morning the clearing is empty.

I paused, not sure where all this stuff was coming from. Possessed was the only way I would have described it; it was as if the story was telling me.

Miss Tish wanted to know if the blue girl was at the meeting. I told her that she was not. Nik wanted to know where they had all gone.

'They have all gone home except the man with the tattoo. He has just walked deeper into the bush.'

'Wasn't the clearing here, in the Lerderderg?' Anna didn't miss a trick. I thought, thank you, Anna.

'It sure is.'

There was a bemused silence; the epic was about to join us at the campfire. The epic had been dwelling in a parallel world—now we were about to meet our opposite number.

The silent axe-murderer was out there, listening to us. He had, it seemed, a tattoo on his forehead. I had the opportunity to rewrite the week, so I began. I sat on the tallest stump and deliberately used a voice that would be heard beyond the circle of the fire. I was addressing the night, the axe-murderer and something beyond that I didn't understand myself. I guess my story was a way of getting the silent axe-murderer to explain.

The silent walker is sitting by the river when the big two-tone green bus pulls up. He watches as fourteen teenagers and three adults collect their packs and head up the river path. He follows and waits. He is amazed at the size of the load each carries. His own swag lies across his shoulders. He sees them break into a sweat as soon as they start walking. He walks coolly through this mild sunshine. It seems they have no wish to progress; they are constantly stopping; one girl collapses after a couple of hours. The rest of the group take the time to swim; they go through elaborate rites of changing, they take it in turns to find a partner, then they go down the track and put on shiny swimsuits that are so well fitted that they may as well be wearing nothing.

The silent one is fascinated. He finds these creatures alien, another species. The thing that upsets him most is the noise. He stays as far away as possible, but cannot stand the harshness of the sound or the violence of the language.

He is familiar with the crude language of miners and labourers. They are obscene and take the micky out of everything, but they respect each other. The violent verbal aggro of these creatures he finds far more distressing and sadly foreign. It seems right that the one he seeks should be with such a group. Nothing would excuse the crime that was to come, but it had become understandable.

The tone of the voices only begins to improve at the end of the day when the conversation becomes so quiet that he needs to move closer to the camp to hear it. He paints his face and creeps toward the fire to hear the creation of the blue girl; this is what he has come for, but it puzzles him. The story is told with ritual and hushed tones. There is great eagerness to share the story. Several stories could develop but each teller is careful to respect what has gone before, ignoring other ideas and following the blue girl's story.

When they saw him he ran. There was as yet no reason for him to interfere. He had been pursued

*before—indeed he had always been treated as outcast,
chased into the fringes. With the endurance built from
thousands of country miles he outlasted the beefy
Maori warrior, then, as he had done so many times
before, stepped into the trees and disappeared. Before
Big Bill was on the track to the crossing the silent one
with the blue gecko tatt was pulling his blanket over
his shoulders. Below the ridge he slept on, he could see
the glow of the fire, the scattered tents and the dim figure of the shaven-headed Mr Mungrel nodding in the
glow.*

*The next night he sat on the river stones below the
camp and listened to the next part of the story, but this
time he was more careful not to be seen. Because he is
used to the dark, he doesn't count on our torches or his
wet footprints giving him away. He would have been
more careful if he had witnessed the violence later in
the night that left one of the group with a smashed-in
face.*

A guilty smile escaped me. The others
laughed. This was fun but I wasn't going to allow
anyone to interrupt. I hurried on...

*The third night, tonight, he sits and smiles. He has
no ego, just a job to do, but to hear these young people
tell his own story is a rare moment of humour. Stories
hold no mystery for him; it is no surprise that his own
story has arranged to have itself told. His story, that of*

*the girl and the story of the school group are now so
intertwined that the telling of one adds a chapter to the
others. No story stands alone; one story begins the
next, the telling itself a new story. Stories are simply
the canvas on which we paint our lives—more, they are
the very fabric of consciousness.*

I had no idea where all this bull was coming
from, but I remember it exactly. I felt high as a
kite, I could feel the story spinning towards its
conclusion, and I'd only had a vague idea where
it was leading. I had simply meant to revive the
story and maybe stir Matt up. I had tried him
and convicted him; it seemed the story now
wanted to execute him. My voice is louder now; I
must make sure the man beyond the firelight can
hear.

*The silent man sitting in the bush looks grim as
he listens to my chant about story. He is more than a
little responsible for the prayer; he silently mouths the
words as I recite it again:*

*No story stands alone. One story begins the
next, the telling itself a new story—the very fabric of
consciousness.*

*He settles himself again. He is still listening for a
part of the story that he has already missed. The death
of the blue girl was told by the redhead during the
afternoon when he was too far away to hear.*

I am racing now. I career on recklessly. The story must find its ending. I suddenly feel like a traitor.

It is not until he hears my last line, the very line that I have just uttered, when I tell about the bit of the story where the blue girl is run down by a Volkswagen … I stood and pointed at Matt … *It is not until I say that Matt killed off the story that he realises who committed the crime. It is not until I tell these things, utter these truths that he understands the crime that he came to hear has already been committed. He steps from the trees, the time has come—*

'You're a fucking wanker.' Matt had been staring at the fire. Now he looked at me, 'A fucking wanker,' he muttered. 'What do you expect me to do, take it back, change the events? It's … it's just a story, just a stupid story …' He stared at the group, looking for support. 'This is bullshit!'

'Why take it so personally then, Matt?' Miss Tish wanted to know. 'And can you do me the courtesy of watching your language. I think it's a terrific story.'

Matt wasn't paying attention to her. He was looking at the man.

It was then that we all noticed the figure standing at the edge of the clearing. He was really still. The whole clearing looked like the freeze frame on the video. For a minute I actually expected him to have a tattoo on his forehead but he didn't. He looked like he was waiting for something, a bus or the lights to change. He didn't look like he had just stepped out of the bush, he didn't look right. He was amused by something, there was a smile around the corners of his mouth. He didn't even look at us, he was looking past us off into the bush. I was stuffed, I couldn't move, I felt like I had conjured him, I was responsible, I just didn't know how to get rid of him. The epic that had moments before filled my mind to the point of obsession had evaporated.

Then he was gone. I could hear the group starting to breathe again. I was surprised that no one had run screaming into the night, but I guess the dark was scarier than the fireside.

I was really angry, confused. If it had been the same guy as the first night I wouldn't have worried too much—I had pretty much convinced myself that he was pretty harmless. This guy didn't have the thin face—I was pretty sure the shape of the face and the hair weren't right—plus this guy was much bigger. There was more than one stranger out there.

Part of me wanted to scream, 'What is it out there, how many bastards are there out there?' The thought that we had no idea about who, or how many were out in the bush made me want to chuck up. All of me wanted Mungrel and Big Bill to walk into camp right then.

Instead of teachers walking into camp a student was walking out. Matt, stick in hand, brushed past me as he strode after the visitor. He was really pissed off. He didn't even answer when I called after him. It seemed he wanted to confront the visitor and find out what the hell was going on. He said later he was angry with me but that what was eating him most was that we were victims in someone's game. We had been trapped, helpless, stalked, living with the fear and uncertainty, the awful powerlessness. I wanted to know what was going on, too. When I'd had time to think about it I realised that I was really angry but I wouldn't have gone off into the night on my own. Once I realised Matt was going regardless of what I said, I knew that I would follow. I'd done it, in the blink of an eye, from a standing start; I'd gone from wishing the teachers were there to charging into the night. I realise now I would not have done it at the start of that week but three days in the Lerdy and I was going to demand an explanation. I hadn't gone far when I wished I'd grabbed a stick, but I guess the sight of Adam's smashed face was pretty fresh in my mind.

It was, after all, my fault Matt was so angry. I wasn't going to let him face this guy alone. We had no idea who or what this guy was. I didn't count on Becc chasing me. Everything happened so fast we didn't really hear Miss Tish, Becc or Kelly and they reckoned they'd yelled themselves sick. Then Becc had just come sprinting after me—that was kinda cool, stupid but cool.

I was twenty metres into the bush, just getting my night vision, just keeping track of Matt when I realised there was someone behind me. My heart stopped. I spun. It was only Becc. I didn't want to send her back, didn't want to leave her alone—at the same time I didn't want to lose track of Matt. I was already in no man's land. I either had to slink back to camp or make sure I didn't lose Matt. I grabbed Becc's hand and we barrelled on in the direction I thought Matt had gone.

I knew in the back of my mind that if we lost track of where the camp was we would be stuck out here all night. I also thought that if Matt came across the stranger before we got to him he would have to deal with him alone and Matt was a midget compared to this bloke. I had one moment of clarity when I cursed Matt, myself, the teachers and the whole school thing for being such idiots. I had visions and a moment of the shakes. I vividly pictured an evacuation helicopter rescuing us, the press telling the world how dead we were or worse what idiots we had been. Then I got angry, I remember being angry with the strangers in the bush as we kept following what seemed to be a faint track, hoping like crazy that none of the crowd of night stalkers would turn out to be real axe-murderers.

It felt like we were walking for ages; it seemed further because I was aware of getting further and further from the camp. In my hesitation when Becc found me we had lost sight of Matt so we were travelling in the hope that we would eventually catch up and that he hadn't left the track. It was too dark to be sure of your footing and it was getting steeper as we got closer to the wall of the gorge so we couldn't run. All afternoon I had been wishing I was alone with Becc. Now I had my wish. Mum always says, 'Be careful what you wish for in case your wish comes true.'

Miss Tish was the one to start the epic up again, Anna told me later. They had no sooner stopped shouting than Miss Tish muttered, '*In loco parentis*. I am supposed to take the same care a parent would; your parents would not have let you go running after some stranger in the bush. You heard me try and stop them?' She looked around hopefully. 'You all heard me, there was nothing I could do. They just wouldn't listen. I can't go after them; I shouldn't leave you guys alone out here.' This was the first time that anybody had heard Miss Tish lose it.

'Where do you think the guy came from?' Anna asked her. 'It wasn't the same one was it?'

Tish's tiny bit

Knowing my luck he will turn out to be an axe-murderer,' Miss Tish said. *He'll take them deep into the bush and chop them all into little pieces and I'll have to go and tell their parents that it was all my fault.*

end Tish's li'l bit

It seems by then she had forgotten she was supposed to be keeping the troops calm.

'Mungrel's in charge, isn't he? He's responsible. You've done real good, Miss. You've been on your own most of the time.' Kelly tried to make people feel good, as usual. 'We shouldn't have been left on our own. Mungrel said they would be here by dark—well where are they?'

Then Dicko decided to clear up the mystery. 'That guy was no axe-murderer. It's probably just a joke.' Dicko does have a weird sense of humour.

Dicko's version

They walk out into the bush and... Without realising it he began telling the next chapter of the epic. People were distracted and only half listening, but they drifted towards the fire. Dicko went on... *They find a campfire. The three of them, Matt, Stu and Becc see the light up ahead and creep cautiously toward the fire. They hear voices, men's voices. They spread out and crawl forward. They are really cautious and quiet. As they get closer to the fire the voices stop. They peer into the campsite but it is deserted.*

They are lying there wondering what happened to the men when they hear the sound of laughter out beyond the shadows. They freeze. What the hell, they think. They begin to crawl away from the fire but there is laughter behind them. They are trapped. They lie there whispering at each other, sorry that they left the safety of the group. Forgotten now is their idea to grab this guy and demand to know what is going on.

Then a face appears, illuminated by a torch. It is gross and appears to hang in the air; now it is laughing at them. It is the face from the first night—the haunted look, and the tufty-looking hair. Becc lets rip this amazing scream. They stand to run and run smack into the strong arms of strangers. The strangers grab them and haul them into the light of the fire. They are struggling like crazy but can't break the grip of the men, who are laughing.

'Would you like a cuppa?' one asks. 'The billy's boiled.'

They are released and the two men move to sit by the fire, still chuckling and looking at the three victims of their joke. The third man arrives from behind them; his face it seems was the floating one that had scared them witless just moments before. He is wearing camouflage army gear, which explains why he looked bodiless. They have been the victims of a joke; they had been lured and then set up. The joke was apparently over. They had been released; they were it seemed free to go, but were welcome to stay.

'What do you think you're doing?' Matt had found his voice first.

'Scaring the shit out of you.' It was the little guy in the army gear. He was obviously enjoying himself.

'Who are you?' Becc wanted to know.

'Who are we? We're ex-students; we first came out here about six years ago. Mungrel brought us out on a four-day hike; we've been coming back ever since.'

'Why pick on us—why stuff up our camp? Is this what you do every year?'

'No!' It was the taller one. 'It was just a coincidence you were out here at the same time. We usually play some war games—y'know, skirmish n'stuff. You guys were just in the way. Span here,' he motioned toward the little guy, 'crept up on you the first night cause he thought you were us. We didn't mean to scare you, but it was pretty funny.'

'What happened to your teachers?' Span wanted to know. 'What happened to Big Bill Tuwhati and Mungrel? Weren't they with you that first night? Big Bill chased me, but then what happened? They didn't get lost did they? Mungrel should know his way around by now.'

'It's a long story,' Matt began. 'And it's your fault.'

Matt gave them the run-down of events from when Span had done his face-at-the-edge-of-the-firelight trick all the way through to the three of them running out into the night.

The three guys, while not too upset, were apologetic at the trouble that they had caused. 'We were just trying to make your walk a little more entertaining,' *the larger guy explained. 'I bet Mungrel wants to kill us. He's getting a bit old to be running up and down these hills.'*

Dicko looked around like he had just taken care of all our problems. 'And that is my part of the epic.'

end Dicko's bit

Sarah was not impressed. 'Because you tell a story doesn't make it true. I don't know how you can tell a story while they're out there with at least two lunatics. I could tell a story where this guy who walks out of the bush gives me a million dollars but that doesn't mean it's going to happen. Matt, Stu and Becca just got themselves worked up. They started to confuse the epic with what's real. If they were thinking right they wouldn't go off into the bush at night.'

Anna said she thought then that reality is just what we perceive it to be. It only exists in our minds. Sometimes we share realities but mostly we live in separate worlds. These worlds are simply just what we think they are and that the whole camp might just have been someone's dream.

But Miss Tish said, 'I hope Nigel is right and this has all been part of some very sick joke.'

No one ever called Dicko Nigel, not even his teachers. Everybody just stared out into the shadows, Anna said; probably all trying to work out their own versions of what was really happening.

Then Kelly leant forward into the firelight. 'Okay, my turn,' she said. 'What you guys don't understand is that as of this afternoon Stuart the stud and Becc are in lust. She told me! This is what is really happening out there.'

Kelly's bit

Stuart and Becc end up together. As they walk deeper into the night, Becc starts to grow more frightened; she walks closer and closer.

This was the only part of the story that Kelly had attempted, and Anna said you could tell she was enjoying herself—this was her kind of story. Even if Matt was lost in the night bush she couldn't resist a bit of romance.

Stuart is intent on finding Matt but Matt is too far ahead. They stumble on not sure if they are still on the track. They can just see someone moving ahead of them. They hurry towards the figure. They assume it to be Matt but enter a clearing to find the figure gone. They stand there in the gloom, Becc clinging to Stuart. He is aware of her warmth in the dark, he can hear her

*breathe, imagines he hears her heartbeat, he leans
down, his lips searching for hers, they meet then part
slightly. Becc's arms let go of Stuart's arm and without
breaking the kiss slides into a full embrace, their bodies
straining against each other. Where is the fear that
riveted them? It is now welding them together. Stuart
holds Becc's face in his hands and drinks long of her
lips. Her hands roam Stuart's back, as if she wants to
experience all of him at once. The hunger that was
kindled that afternoon threatened to devour them
now. Stuart's hands explored Becc's shoulders, her
waist, her hips, her butt. With his hands clamped to her
backside Stuart leans away from Becc's hungry lips,
'Wow,' he whispers. Becc lifts his hands away from her
butt and clamps them desperately to her breasts, 'I
want you,' she demands.*

*Stuart drops to his knees and begins to explore her
breasts and get her skivvy untucked…*

Kell is breathless but Miss Tish's voice breaks
in…

*Then she becomes rigid with fear. She is staring
over his head. He looks to see what it is.*

Anna said the whole group groaned. Miss
Tish had taken over the story just when it was getting really horny.

'Go on then, what is she looking at?' Tanja
wanted to know.

Becc realised that there was a faint light coming from the cliff, from inside the cliff. They move to the cliff and move into the mouth of a cave, the light emanates from the tunnel that leads off into the hill.

end Kell's bit

'Is there a bed in the cave?' Dicko wanted to know.

'I'll finish the sexy version later Dicko, just for you, okay?' Kelly seemed a bit browned off that she had been censored. 'This tunnel better be more interesting than my Becc does Stu.' She was giving Miss Tish a greasy but I don't think she would have been too serious.

I've asked Tish a couple of times since, what was supposed to happen in the tunnel but somehow she never got around to telling it. I reckon she only wanted to stop the X-rated version. She didn't have any clear idea where the story was going. It didn't matter because there were enough stories out there bumping into each other already. It was amazing that there was an element of truth in her bit about the tunnel. I guess there was a bit of lust, too. Anyway she didn't get to finish her bit of the epic because it was then that Becc and I staggered back into camp. The truth of the matter was that we had wandered around in the dark for a while too petrified to go far from the fire. We'd lost Matt almost as soon as he got into the bush; he went too fast and we went too slow.

That was our story anyway. That's what we told the group, that nothing had happened. But we lied. We didn't tell the truth because we thought part of it was private and part of it we felt a bit guilty about. That makes it sound like we did IT, but we didn't. It didn't seem to matter at the time if we didn't tell the truth. Most of it was private anyway.

As I said we lost Matt almost as soon as we got out into the bush—even with Becc's torch we couldn't move fast enough to keep up. And we did wander about. We walked up hill following the creek to see if we could see the campfire from higher up. We also thought we might see Matt. Instead we found not a cave or a tunnel as Tish had used in her epic but the mouth of a collapsed mine.

We were sitting there in the moonlight talking and looking down at the silvery river below when we realised we were sitting on the stones of a fireplace. The stones had been scattered a bit but they were really black and when I kicked at them with my boot there was this great plume of ash. It seemed strange because no one would camp this far from the river when there was a great spot just above the river.

As we looked around I noticed a ramp leading down into the cliff. It looked like a wombat hole. Since I'd never heard of wombats lighting campfires I was a bit curious. I realised as I walked right up to the dirt wall that it was covered by a piece of hessian; in fact the hessian was disguising the opening to a horizontal mineshaft. Someone had thrown dirt over the hessian to make it look like a part of the cliff wall.

We stood just inside the mouth of the dwelling wondering about the occupant. We felt we were trespassing. We didn't discuss looking around. I guess we felt we had a right to know who had been driving us nuts all week. There was actually a fireplace at the back of the room with a neat stone chimney. There were shelves on the walls and a sapling bed piled with flattened bracken fronds. In fact the whole place was neat as a pin. Our first thought was that it was an old prospector's hut, but the wood of the bed had been hacked through recently. We stood wondering if it was the home of the axe-murderer. There was actually a hand axe by the fire. There were billies piled neatly, a plastic wash tub. There was a hurricane lantern suspended from the roof and books on the shelf of driftwood above the bed. There was a backpack and a folded tent at the foot of the bed. I groped in the top of the backpack as Becc looked at the books with the torch. I pulled out a handful of clothes and found I was holding a black bra and a couple of pairs of knickers. I called Becc over to bring the torch.

'This guy is very kinky. He collects ladies' underwear.'

'What makes you think it's a guy?' She showed me the name in the front cover of the book. I put the clothes back in the pack.

'That guy we saw the first night. He couldn't have been a girl, could he?'

'He had short hair but that means nothing. Is that name familiar?' She opened the book again and went back to the shelf above the bed.

'That face was covered in clay or something... because the name is in the book doesn't mean it's her.'

Becc was sitting on the bed with the torch reading from a small hardback book. It was black with red corners and filled with handwritten entries.

'It's a diary of some sort.' Becc closed the book and looked at me. I kissed her. I couldn't help it.

We both knew we had no right to read the diary but we did anyway. What can I say? We were so curious we couldn't have not read it. We wanted to know who had stalked us, who lived in the mineshaft. At least, we read the first couple of pages until Becc's torch decided we should read no more.

the diary begins...

Ah Kow's Ruin

I've been here three days. I'm starting to realise what I've done. I'm not going back.

I've not spoken to anyone for five days. No, I did tell the sulphur-crested cockies to shut up when they woke me at first light again. The silence is wonderful.

I'll have to head out to the shop at Greenvale in a couple of days. I'm running out of food. I wonder if I can do my shopping without saying anything. I wonder if I should ring Dad but then I'd have to talk. I left him a note, which should be enough. I really don't want to talk, especially to him. I guess I'm not Daddy's little girl any more.

Words equal lies! A world full of lies. I have decided to take a vow of silence. I will never speak again.

I've been talking to the trees! So much for my vows.

Lies and silence. It's either lies or they refuse to talk, so much is taboo. No one talked about Mark. We didn't get to say goodbye.

You don't need to talk. I did my shopping, and all I had to do was smile and nod my head. Automatic tellers actually encourage us not to talk. I got a bigger billy for cooking which I really needed. I even bought a hat at the op shop. It's cool. It's like an old bowls hat—it even says Emberton on the band. I was stuffed. I figure it's about fifteen Ks to Greenvale and back.

It was even further because I stayed on the road so no one would see me sneak back into the bush. I had a meat pie. They are usually disgusting, but this one was brilliant. Probably because I didn't have to cook it on a campfire. I bought some meat this time. Three weeks without meat was too much. I have no way of keeping it cold. I'll have to eat it within a couple of days, before it goes off. It's still mostly dehydrated stuff, yucko.

I've been thinking about Ah Kow. He's the Chinaman this place is named for or after. I wonder if he was alone, too. He was tough. You should see the stone he moved. He actually changed the course of the river.

It took me a while to work out exactly what he had done but he was able to build a race that diverted the river so that he could mine the bed of the river and or wash the dirt. His hole is why I have such a wonderful swimming hole. I sat in the sun naked for the first time. I've always been worried about someone coming, especially on the weekends when bush walkers might be out and about. I've never felt so free—freedom, silence and sunshine. I felt so good—sublime pleasure, if that is the right word. Sitting here on my rock, I realised I can't remember the last time I felt really happy.

I got lost yesterday. God it was scary! I was following these wallabies, a mother and young one. I was rapt to see them so close in the wild and I just followed them as they moved on. I was further from the river than I've dared go before. I seem to do things in a trance since I went bush.

Someone gets lost in this gorge every year. It's killed people. I wandered about. The hills slant in all directions—you think you're headed for the river but you're just going around in circles. I felt alone for the first time since I ran away. I sat down and cried for ages. It's been a long time since I cried like that, yet

I've felt like it so often—I used to cry at the drop of a hat, when I was small. When I was all cried out, I just sat there and relaxed. I stopped thinking about it, pretended that it didn't matter. It didn't somehow.

I realised I was east of the river, so if I waited till the sun started going down, I should run towards the sunset. If I was fast enough I should get back to the river, if not, I'd just spend a night without my gear. I had matches—I wouldn't freeze or die in the night.

That was enough. It was that simple. Life and death. I can't believe I was so uptight a couple of weeks ago—it seems like a lifetime. Almost like these aren't the same eyes. I feel more alive today. My tent is a Taj, Ah Kow's clearing my world.

It was the end of a page, but the torch was about to give out and we still needed to get back to camp.

We put everything back just how we'd found it. But we knew who Mark was. We knew the writer was someone from our school and we knew that he wore bras—well we knew it was a girl and she had run away. We weren't sure that this was the person who we had seen by the campfire light that first night—in fact it looked unlikely. I couldn't imagine a girl bolting through those prickles. They are really solid and the spikes just rip straight into you. I just couldn't come at the idea that a girl had been out here for weeks, all by herself, even after the diary told me otherwise. Becc said it sounds sexist but I couldn't put the lace bra and the haunted face we'd seen in the firelight together.

We even put the hessian back in place and covered it in dirt again. We felt guilty about invading the hide-out and reading the diary so we decided not to tell. We figured that the girl was no threat so the group didn't need to know about the mine dwelling. The whole trip from the time we followed Matt away from the campfire had been extraordinary. Becc had told me a story and I had told her one. No, I'm not going to tell either of those stories.

It was pretty special. By the time we got back to the group we were pretty close and we didn't feel like sharing that either. How can you share what it is like to fall in love?

I was scared. I still couldn't believe that Becc would really want to go out with me. Then she said something that took for granted that we were going out, like she'd already decided. Then the moon came out. The night went from being dark and threatening to a magical world bright with silver. So did my life.

I felt a bit guilty when we got back because I wasn't too worried and everyone else was. I guess I had forgotten about the other bloke that had turned up at the fire and I'd forgotten Matt.

The group, Anna mostly, filled us in on the epic. We were pretty sheepish because our real epic had been better than the ones they made up.

I wasn't going to let the epic die there. Little old Miss Ralph at school always reckons you shouldn't let the facts get in the way of a good story. So I thought about telling them the next episode of the epic where the guy with the blue gecko on his forehead abducts Matt and takes him to Nik's sandstone wall. I guess I was just too spooked. I was scared that Matt might really have been abducted. I was amazed that they had been telling the epic at all. We had been worried about Big Bill while he was missing, but Matt was another matter. He was just a kid, no match for the man that we had all seen clearly at the fire. And even if Becc and I knew about the girl we still had no idea of what was really happening.

Miss Tish grilled us about what had happened but we were helpless; there was nothing we could do, except wait. Miss Tish kept muttering about us being stupid. I think she was glad to see us but was really worried about Matt.

She'd been worried enough, done enough waiting, for one week.

◉

Matt's pretty quiet at school, but last year on the basketball trip to Mildura he became this one-man terrorist squad. He doesn't play much sport but he's pretty good at basketball. We almost had to beg him to come so we had a team. He had this green wool beanie hat and big green, wrap-around sunnies, green rubber gloves he found in the back of the van and that old derro coat he wears. Bourkie's dad has this Bedford van with a sliding sun roof. He calls it the Shaggin' Wagon; Bourkie calls it something that rhymes with truck, but his dad only uses it for his plumbing supplies business. Anyway we're flying around Mildura with Matt standing on the seat, head and shoulders out the roof, flapping his arms. Mr Bourke was cacking himself, driving like an idiot. We've parked outside this fish and chip shop. Matt hasn't got his gear on but there is this nice looking girl waiting outside the shop. Matt says 'Hi' on the way in then on the way out he whispers to her, 'beware the Green Hornet'. We get back into the van, he whips on the green stuff and pops out the roof and stands there really still, looking at her through the green wrap-around glasses, with the green hat, green gloves and Matt's freckled manic grin. She doesn't notice him for a minute and then she literally falls down in shock, then can't get up because she's giggling too hard. It was magic.

Then as we drive along he starts up this noise like the whine of a fighter plane in a dive. We stop at the lights, Matt leaps out of the side door, sounding like a screaming jet. He runs like an emu with his arms held back like wings and great loping strides, knees way up, screams up to this old girl waiting at the pedestrian lights, gives her a big kiss and screams back to the van. We tear away from the lights with Matt back in position; he gives the old girl this huge grin as he flies by. The next day the Green Hornet was seen all over Mildura, not to mention the basketball stadium. We've changed the name of our team for next year; we are now the Green Hornets. On the way home we called into Macca's. We drive through, order our food and as we pull away Matt tells the girl in the headset to beware of the Green Hornet. We knew what was coming, we drive out, Matt jumps into his gear, runs back through the drive-in lane, grabs this girl, leans her back Hollywood style and kisses her. Then screams off up the driveway. We didn't even see it but we laughed about it all the way home. Even though he still wears the green hat Matt got tired of the Green Hornet after the Mildura trip; I thought we'd seen the last of that elusive superhero.

The mood at the campfire was pretty grim. Becc and I were happy but Miss Tish sure wasn't. Mungrel and Big Bill still hadn't shown. Matt was still out in the bush somewhere chasing some strange guy who liked frightening school groups out of their skull, and Miss Tish was probably still worried about the yella fella who had been stalking us all week and was out there too. The clouds had broken up as the evening went on until we had a whole sky full of stars. It should have been cold like the previous two nights out in the gorge but there was this gentle northerly breeze. It was really mild, then this huge orange moon laboured over the side of the gorge. The moon was like someone had turned the lights on; you could even see the distant shape of Mt Blackwood. When the moon first came up you had the feeling that you could just about reach up and touch it. It was really bright; you didn't need a torch even though it was one in the morning. The fire wasn't as cosy, didn't seem so safe, you could see a long way but there were these chunks of shadow that could hide anything. Some went to bed; others just sat around quietly waiting.

Becc and I wandered down to the bank of the river. It was just below the campsite, well in earshot if you called out, so Miss Tish was cool. If you stood up near the track you could see us from the tents. Becc remarked how appropriate it was that the moon had come out and I said, 'Why?' She said it was romantic. I said, 'Is it? I reckon it's kinda spooky. It makes everyone look like they're dead, they get these shadows in their eye sockets.' Then she kissed me and I thought the moon was really romantic.

That's when we heard the screaming jet.

'What's that?' Becc wanted to know.

'Not what. Who. It's the Green Hornet! It's Matt!'

It sounded a long way off but we knew the Green Hornet rode again. It was cool to know Matt was okay. Better still you knew that if he was the Green Hornet he was invulnerable. He was in charge. He was the last of the Superheros—at least he thought he was.

'It's the Green Blowfly,' chortled Dicko as he came racing down the bank. 'Yeah, it's the Green Hornet. Matt's all right!'

I realise now that I'd actually expected the story to take its revenge on Matt. I was confused to find that he was all right. The whole thing had an unreal feel to it. In reality I hoped and expected Matt to be okay. But the story was in my brain, mixing up what I thought. Finding the runaway girl's hut and diary had also confused me. I didn't know what was going on but it spurred me to do something. I wanted to go and find Matt. I had a feeling he might have found the girl from the diary. I wanted to know who he was making screaming jet noises for. If he just wanted us to know he was safe he could have just yelled out. He was doing a number on someone else. He was trying to freak someone out. I wanted to know who.

'Neeeeouwwww!' Matt was getting closer. The river was shallow, wide and noisy; it seemed to dodge back and forward between the bottom of alternating ridges. We were on the right-hand bend but could see the ridge that was the left-hand turn on the other side of the river further upstream; the bush was thinner on the ridge. Only because of the sound of the Green Hornet we were able to pick out the dark blob that was Matt's beanie dodging down through the trees. Once we picked out Matt we could see that he was shadowing someone. It was the guy that had appeared at the fire. He had almost reached the river. This meant he was almost out of sight again. It looked like Matt was still chasing that guy. I guess we were fearful he would be the one getting chased. It was then Becc spotted the other one—the yella fella from the first night—much closer to us, again on the other side of the river. Miss Tish and the others that hadn't gone to sleep had joined us by now.

We pointed out where Matt had been and where the others had disappeared. We could see no one by then. Miss Tish kept saying no one was to leave the camp. The Green Hornet had gone quiet. We stood for ages just watching and listening. We were standing there in moonlit silence, watching the silver river. It was whispering away like Mrs Noy at school; she never raises her voice and when she starts whispering everyone seems to get quieter, calmer somehow.

It seemed like a silent movie—I guess because we could only hear the river. Then the guy Matt had been chasing came running out of the bush on the other side of the river and just ran across the ford, knee deep. He ran up to the group and asked where our teacher was. We all looked at Tish. She was standing there with her sleeping bag wrapped around her and I swear she looked younger than most of us.

'I need a rope. One of your kids is down a mineshaft!'

The Green Hornet had gone underground. There was discussion about the rope we didn't have. It turned out later that Mungrel had a rope in his pack but Tish didn't know and no one thought to look. Dicko was pissed off; he'd carried Mungrel's pack as well as his own most of that day. In the end the guy pulled the flies off three tents and tied them together and then bolted back across the river, followed by all of us. He stopped long enough to tell us to stay well back; the ground was really loose. Matt was perched on a log jammed in a concealed shaft. If the log slid down we would never be able to reach him. Someone had pulled the wings off the Green Hornet.

We stumbled, splashed, tiptoed across the river and followed the guy with his bundle of tent flies up the track, upstream, along a faint track. We must have looked a ragged collection. As we hovered around the guy lay down on the track and lowered the flysheets into a hole in the grass. There is no way anyone would have spotted that there was a shaft there. The guy said it sounded like the earth covering the entrance had caved in when he had thrown Matt off him. It seems Matt had decided that the big guy was chasing the little guy we had seen the first night. He'd seen him grab the smaller guy and the smaller guy had struggled to get away. Becc and I were pretty convinced by now that the little guy was the yella fella, the girl who wrote the diary.

Matt had been trying to give the little guy time to get away, hence the screaming jet imitations. There was no way that the bloke could creep up on the smaller bloke with the Green Hornet hovering or should I say dive-bombing. Matt said that they had just about caught up with the smaller guy so he had jumped out in front of the big guy, only to be flung into the bush. The big guy was really keen to get at the little guy. He kept calling him some girl's name, saying he just wanted to talk.

We didn't know all this as we held our breath above the shaft. Matt called, 'I've got it!... ah shit... the log moved. Pull me up.'

The guy looked up at us. 'Okay. I want a couple of you to give me a hand. We have to pull him out nice and smooth.' And then he shouted into the hole, 'Have you got a good hold?'

'Yeah. Pull me up.'

The guy had the tail of the fly wrapped around his fists. It was just as well, it was really hard to get a good grip. I was hoping Matt had a good hold. As we started pulling on the fly there were these sick tearing noises. I guess it was only the nylon stretching under the strain. I needn't have worried. One haul and we had him out full length on the track, unknotting his knuckles from the twists of fly material. Most of the hole was covered by grass so that as we hauled him out Matt really looked like a very pale Green Hornet leaving its nest.

I remember really clearly that as he untangled his hands they began to flutter like butterflies that had just been released. He couldn't control them. He looked a bit embarrassed and put his hands between his thighs. He said later that when the log slipped a couple of rocks fell into the darkness. All he could see was a glimmer of moonlight at the top of the shaft and flashes from our torches. All he could think about he said was what if they couldn't get his body out, what if the whole shaft collapsed? He could hear us thumping about above him. The whole time he'd wanted to throw up; he'd knackered himself when he landed on the log. One minute he was the Green Hornet, the last of the Superheros;

next he was underground, one step above the void, with his testicles keeping company with his Adam's apple.

I guess I was underestimating the feeling of drama we had before Matt fell into the shaft. But as they say it's all relative. Matt's real drama was far worse than the ones we had been imagining. The guy we were freaked about was a hero. He'd saved Matt's life. True, it had been him that had flung Matt out of the way and into the shaft, but it had been an accident. And you don't go to all that trouble to save someone so you can kill him. He didn't look like a bloke that had just saved a life. Actually, he looked like a bloke that had lost the Grail and found a paper cup. He still sat on the track where he'd pulled Matt out, staring at the ground. It was while we were grilling Matt about what had happened that I realised Becc was missing.

Dicko wasn't around either, but I didn't notice that he was gone. I looked down the track and guessed Becc's disappearance had something to do with the other person, the one that had been haunting us all week. Everyone was busy talking to Matt so I did what Becc had done and just quietly drifted down the track heading for the last place we had seen the girl. I was a bit sorry Becc hadn't told me where she was going. Maybe that was why I missed the track that went up along the bank and I ended up at the river where we had just crossed. I could see the fire and thought it weird that it was deserted, but I could hear the rest further around the river, heading back. I didn't want them to catch me so I quickly backtracked and found the faint fork in the track and headed directly uphill. The bank got steeper until it wound along above the river. I discovered a clear ledge, five metres long and ten to fifteen metres directly above the river. As I climbed I got a great view of our camp on the opposite bank and the silver river below.

It was then that I saw the wombat or what I thought was a wombat. The flat area came to a halt at the cliff edge and this wombat was snuffling over the edge and then it disappeared. It didn't look right. And then I heard Dicko yell and I knew what I'd thought was a wombat was really Dicko's backside.

He'd had his knees tucked up under him leaning over the edge. In the moon shadow Dicko's backside covered his feet. Once his backside took off I saw his boots, then they too disappeared over the edge, and then came Dicko's cry of alarm as he plummeted towards the river. He only bounced once before he hit the water. Luckily he only bruised a few ribs.

I'd imagined that Becc had shot through from the group after we got Matt out of the hole. But she didn't even follow us up the track. Dicko was with us but noticed Becc fade back and scoot up the other track, so after Matt was safe Dicko followed her.

Becc said that she was so focused on the diary girl all along that when she had the chance to follow her she just took off. I was a bit miffed. She should have told me; it could have been dangerous. She just says I'm trying to be a macho man.

Becc said she caught up to the girl really quickly because she had kept an eye on her while we were talking to the guy about rescuing Matt. It was easy for Becc to follow her in the bright moonlight. It was just as well, because even right on her tail she lost her at the cliff edge.

She hunted around the cliff for a while. There was nowhere else anyone could have gone unless it was right over the edge. She got down and shone her torch over the edge and discovered a small ledge just big enough to stand on. There were a couple of tree roots to hold on to, so she lowered herself over the edge and onto the ledge. She looked straight down to the river. There was nowhere to go. As she turned to climb back up she discovered a cleft in the rock behind the ledge; it opened out into a cave. She flashed her torch inside but couldn't see anything, so she scrambled inside and found that the cave was a couple of metres wide and deep, one and a half high. She said that that was when her heart stopped; there in the torchlight sat the girl with an open Swiss army knife and the wildest look in her eyes, obviously scared to death. I would have dived back out of that cave if someone had pointed a knife at me. Becc said she tried to talk to her, tell her that she wouldn't hurt her. It wasn't until she swore that she wouldn't tell anyone where she was that the girl lowered the blade.

Becc says she asked lots of questions but got no response from the girl until she asked about the other person that we had met that night, the one that had thrown Matt down a mineshaft. She started asking if he was trying to hurt her. No response. Did she know him? No response. Is he your dad? The girl nodded slowly; the guy was her dad and she had been running away from him. Becc asked again if he wanted to hurt her and she shook her head. Becc asked if he wanted to talk to her. She nodded. But you don't want to talk to him, a shake. Has he hurt you? Again a shake. You don't want to talk to anyone? The girl in the torchlight determinedly shook her head.

Becc was tossing up what to do next when she heard the noise of Dicko thumping about above the cave. The girl reacted instantly moving towards the cave mouth with the knife ready. Becc whispered that it was all right, she would go and send them away. She was worried about someone getting stabbed so she was desperate when climbing out of the cave to keep everyone away. It was then she found what she thought was her whistle, hanging down on its cord above the cave mouth. It must have caught on a root when she lowered herself over the edge, she figured. She spotted it in the moonlight, grabbed it and pulled. Dicko shot past her, bounced on the ledge and flew off into the river below. Then Becc realised that her whistle, the one we were all forced to wear in case of emergency, was still under her flanny shirt! The one she had grabbed had, it seemed, been attached to Dicko. She could hear him swearing and splashing below as he floundered in the silver river.

It was then that my head appeared over the edge to see where Dicko and his boots had disappeared to and saw Becc laughing at me. 'Come on, Foo, help me up!' She keeps calling me that. I hadn't even admitted to myself that I was worried about Becc, but it was such a relief to see her safe.

Becc's going to hit me if I say I don't understand women again, ouch! She did. But I don't understand that she could spend five minutes in a cave with this girl and decide to protect her. So, at the time, she just said that she would tell me everything later, and she didn't even tell me until we got back to camp that she had met the girl. She said, later, that was in case we came across the girl's father.

As it was, there was enough confusion when we got back. Matt was sitting by the fire wrapped in a blanket and looking paler than usual, pale green in fact. Mungrel and Big Bill had turned up just in time to find the camp deserted. Then Mungrel said they heard a scream and saw Dicko dive out of the trees into the river. They watched Dicko wading out of the river, holding his ribs, as the rest of the group came back from rescuing Matt from the mineshaft. Miss Tish came wandering back with this strange bloke and with a sleeping bag wrapped around her shoulders.

Mungrel did a count, only to find that Becc and I were missing. The guys carried on when they realised we were out there together. Thankfully, that's when we turned up. Tish introduced the guy; it seemed Mungrel knew him. They shook hands.

'I'm sorry if I spooked you kids,' he began. 'But it's a long story.'

'Well I really think I need a coffee.' Mungrel sounded stuffed. Even though it must have been three in the morning by then Mungrel stoked up the fire and put the billy on. 'Now what the bloody hell has been going on out here?'

'Is Adam all right?' Tish asked. I'd forgotten that that was where Mungrel had been all this time.

'He's in hospital, but his parents are there now. They didn't have to wire up his jaw and the dental surgeon has put most of the teeth back in. He really looked like he'd been hit by a truck last time we saw him. And what were you doing on that cliff, Mr Dickinson?'

Dicko had just returned from changing his clothes. He looked pretty cool with his Pooh Bear sleeping bag wrapped around him and his Mr Bean jim-jams. 'Someone threw me in the river, Mr Mundle.' You have to know Dicko. He said it like he was in court. We just pissed ourselves.

'It was probably my daughter,' the guy declared. He had collected his pack from the bush nearby and was getting out a cup. 'I'm sorry... I don't understand what's happened to her.'

Big Bill was looking at them both. 'You mean a girl picked him up and threw him off the cliff?'

The guy shrugged his shoulders. Dicko looked a bit sheepish.

'Someone pulled my whistle cord and I flipped over the cliff.'

Becc was looking at me and saying nothing so I said nothing. Dicko didn't know who flipped him over the edge.

'Can you show me where?' the guy was onto it straight away.

Then Becc changed her mind.

'Dicko, it was me. I was lost, I saw the whistle hanging over the edge and thought it was mine. I didn't realise you were attached, sorry.' She smiled at Dicko who was rubbing his ribs.

'Lost? How can you be lost when you're hanging in mid-air?' The girl's father had lost interest, which was Becc's intention.

'Where's your daughter now? Still out in the

bush?' Mungrel hadn't caught up with the story yet.

'She's out there somewhere.' He gestured towards the silver hills. 'She ran away three months ago. It seems she has been out here most of that time, living in the bush.'

Mungrel was curious now. 'How did you find her, then?'

'She has been using her key card in Greenvale. I got the bank statement. I went and showed her photo to the shopkeepers and anyone else who might have seen her. I was lucky people in one of the houses next to Mt Blackwood had actually seen her walk down Ah Kow Track. This is the third time I've been out here and this time I saw her ... but she kept running away. I didn't recognise her at first. She's cut off her lovely long hair.'

'Does your daughter often paint her face with yellow clay?' Steph asked. The group was starting to make connections.

'Why did she run away?' Miss Tish wanted to know.

'I don't know.' The man shrugged his shoulders and stared into the flames. 'I don't know why. I've really got no idea. I used to think she was a pretty normal kid.'

It seemed to me that he was pretty upset. I believed him even if Becc didn't. Becc thought there had to be some good reason for someone to run away and live out in the bush.

Miss Tish's question was enough to stop the conversation cold except that Matt explained to Mungrel what had happened to him out in the bush and the guy apologised all over again for throwing him down the shaft. He also apologised for the trouble his daughter had caused during the week. Tish must have told him that we had thought his daughter was some sort of axe-murderer.

So, no one was out there waiting to chop us into little bits. The tension was over and people just collapsed; people's eyes started closing, and when Fei started her cute little snore Mungrel sent us to bed. There was no chance of sharing a tent with Becc so we just hit the sack. I couldn't sleep; three-thirty in the morning, but I wanted to know why the girl wouldn't talk to her dad. Before I dropped off to sleep I had decided that I wanted to read the rest of that diary.

We were pretty slow getting started the next morning; we had till two to get to the bus so we weren't fussed. Most of us didn't wake up until nearly nine. We just cruised around the ruin. I'd been debating about going back to the girl's hut in the mineshaft and reading the diary but I was worried Mungrel would kill me if I went missing. Becc and I were talking about the diary, and had decided to risk it, when the girl's father limped back into camp. He was very pale, probably in shock; his hands were shaking. He had a handkerchief tied around his thigh and there seemed to be a heap of blood on his jeans.

He asked if he could use a first-aid kit. 'Cut myself on a piece of tin,' he offered as Miss Tish handed him the plastic food-container that held the kit. When he took off the handkerchief and pulled back the jeans his leg really bled. Big Bill took over and put some pressure on the wound and got Tanja to get him some water.

'This is pretty deep, you'll need a tetanus shot.'

'I was running,' the guy said. 'I just wanted her to talk to me,' he added.

Becc dragged me away. 'That's a knife wound, it's far too clean and thin. She cut him. She pointed that knife at me.' Becc had seen the Swiss army knife. I had not.

'His daughter? Why?'

'I don't know. She wouldn't talk to me. She doesn't talk. But I'm going to find out.'

I think she said, I'm going to find out; Becc thinks I said it. I can't remember, but I remember both of us slipping from camp and our dash up the hill to where we'd found the mineshaft hut and the diary the day before.

It didn't look like anyone had been into the hut in the side of the hill since we had been there. The hessian was in place and the dirt was neatly spread the way we had left it, but there was lots of blood on the rocks of the old fireplace. I spotted the knife amongst the stones at the foot of the hill. I picked it up and cleaned the blade on a leaf.

We were standing inside, letting our eyes adjust to the gloom, when we heard shouting from down the valley. We ran outside again and realised it was our lot calling to us. They had decided that the girl's father had to have his leg seen to so he needed to walk out with us and if we were going to make it in time we had to get moving to allow for lots of rests.

We looked at each other and Becc said we had to cover the hut again. I feel really guilty about it now, but I said I'd put the knife inside and while Becc waited outside I jammed the diary into my jeans. I guess I knew she wouldn't approve; she didn't. And I was so freaked—I guess because I knew I was doing something piss poor—that I even forgot to put the knife back. So I came out with the knife and the diary. That's why Becc says I've got to take them back.

But she didn't know at the time, so we went back to the group and headed for home.

I was looking forward to some good food and my own soft bed with the hollow bit in the middle but I was a bit sad to be leaving. I'd really enjoyed the camp; even being scared shitless was an adventure. School and home seemed pretty boring. I'd never really been seriously scared before but I had survived. I was more scared about Becc and our feelings for each other now than anything else. I'd been busy trying to hold it together and overcome my fear, but walking out of the gorge I realised I would always be frightened. I remembered how relieved I'd been to see her safe the night before. As long as I cared about anything I would be fearful.

As we climbed out of the gorge I walked beside the girl's limping father. I realised that his fear had to be greater than anything I'd experienced that week. He had taken the trouble to come hunting for his daughter so he must love her. If he loved her then his fear of losing her would have to be terrible. I felt really sorry for him. If she had stabbed him he'd probably lost her. The more you have to lose the greater the fear. I was thinking about his daughter still being out there—the bush, the solitude. To tell the truth I was thinking about being out there with Becc—that wouldn't be solitude though; it'd be heaven.

We were on the four-wheel drive track only a kilometre or two from the bus when Mungrel turned up beside us.

'I want you guys to know, I think you did a really good job.' I realised he'd been talking to everyone in turn.

'I was really scared most of the time.' I told him.

'So was I, petrified. Things were just so out of control. I nearly throttled you for hitting Adam. It really did complicate things.'

'It was your epic that complicated things,' accused Becc.

'Yeah! The characters started turning up in the firelight,' I added.

'What do you mean?' Mungrel grinned but I had a feeling he knew what we were talking about. I remembered when he'd put a hand on my shoulder.

'We'd have to tell you the whole epic.'

'I'd like that, when we get time. You were great. Talk to you later, I want to hear that epic—deal?' Mungrel waved and strode ahead. It was good he was proud of us.

'You know I thought I was scared back there in the bush,' I said to Becc, 'but I think this is scarier, going home. Last weekend I was worried about making it through the week. Now I'm worried about my whole life.' Becc smiled at me.

'You're only scared 'cause now you've got something to lose.'

Like I said I don't understand women but we had been thinking the same thing, now that is scary.

'You know I think I'll miss the epic,' Becc said as she put her arm through mine and we headed for the bus.

I was going to miss the epic too. I'd enjoyed living those lives in my imagination. I felt fit and strong even though I needed sleep. I felt I could survive. I was different out there. I liked the me out there better than the me at home. As soon as I put my pack under the bus and slumped into a seat next to Becc I felt like a kid again. It all seemed a bit of a dream. We slept on each other's shoulders all the way back to school. I dreamt that the camp had been a dream and I felt a bit panicked until I woke and found Becc was still there. It was all true.

I fessed up to Becc on the phone about stealing the diary, the night we got home. She came over straight away even though she was angry with me and we read it together. Becc and I have been arguing about this diary thing ever since and I wasn't going to show anyone, but I have decided to. It is amazing how much it connects with the epic. I don't think the girl would be too upset, in fact I think she might like it published. Her writing sounds like she is writing for someone to read. Plus it looks like it isn't going to make any difference now. Becc convinced me that there are bits of the diary that are private, that have nothing to do with the epic or school, or why the girl was out there at Ah Kow's, so we edited it down to bits that connect with us.

the diary

I keep trying to understand what happened on the last day I went to school. It was a classic spring morning—the sun slung low still, but trying to work its way through the faded curtains. I lay there in the sleepout listening to the flat, hot sound of the magpie warbling about the heat of summer yet to come. A day so wonderful it was almost obscene to contemplate school. It's such a noisy, aggro place. Sometimes I feel violated, sometimes I join in and monster others. Schools smell. I lie here and imagine the smell of the cut spring grass on the ovals and the stench of boys' socks, that stale odour of many bodies, the pong of decay, stagnant minds, old ideas. I can't ever imagine walking up those steps again.

The prospect of school was bad enough. Breakfast was the usual wilderness of tension—the ABC news, the washing machine basely labouring in the bathroom. Out in the pearly blueness the magpie was calling me again, drawing me from under the layers of my morning. It was a song the others couldn't hear. It drew me away from them, from the very language they spoke. Here was a gorge through the middle of the very landscape that was everything I had previously known. Everything seemed new or at least changed. I wondered if I was losing my mind, yet I was so filled with the newness. I felt I could have flown into the sun, where the heat seared away the noise in my head so all I could hear was the heat ticking and the earth shifting minutely as it lay slumbering. Sounds so weird when I write it down—then there was this crow croaking about something.

From then on I felt I was sleep-walking. I went back to the sleepout, for the first time noticing the texture of the fibro. I gathered the books together that I had scattered on the table and then not used. I tried to tie my tie but it felt like a noose. I stuffed it and my blazer into my bag. I must have been on automatic pilot because I headed out the door, I swung the gate closed and noticed the dark, lead-heavy eyes of the house, its red brick brows. It seemed somehow resentful. It seemed insulted by the purple blooms of the jacaranda. I love that tree. I love its name.

I walked down the usual street past other blind houses. They seemed foreshortened. Had I grown in the night? Was change gradual and we just failed to

notice? Was it sudden, overnight, as this transforma-
tion seemed? Had the street changed or had I? I could
see myself perhaps twelve or thirteen labouring up
this same hill beneath a school bag heavy with inno-
cence and expectations, of what? What have they
done to that little girl? Where is she now? She would
have liked the idea of living in a tent then. Why am I
crying again?

I stood back from the two-toned green bus,
unwilling to meet anyone's eyes. I was reluctant to
engage in the push and shove, didn't feel strong
enough but at the same time felt I might kill if pro-
voked. Even my morning smoke didn't calm the tide
of my unease and nausea that grew as the bus
rocked towards the school. By the time we got to the
halfway stop I wanted a second smoke and was
ready to scream at the other kids. Their immature
games, their complacency. They all sat there in near
silence; perhaps they didn't feel the hopelessness,
the emptiness of these small towns, the naked
misery of dead marriages, the veiled violence and
cyclone wire of the schools. I couldn't believe they
weren't aware—they could not see the world I saw,
they didn't know what they were missing. Perhaps
this was real poverty. I felt I could no longer be still,
pretending to be asleep. I could not walk up the
stairs of that school. I could not take the coat and

the tie from the bag. The bus, I knew, went back to the depot. I just stayed on and completed the circle. The driver didn't even notice until I got off and headed back up the hill.

———

The Creek

Fear is a strange thing. I was never really scared when I was living in town, but I was always fearful, fretful. Whenever you're with people you're always expecting them to be at their worst, always looking to take someone down—everyone has their own agenda. Even at home, especially Ursula the Sea Witch. Even if she wasn't the stepmother she'd still be a bitch. Out here there is nothing to fear, nothing has malice; snakes are dangerous, the bush will kill you if you're not careful—like me getting lost the other day—but nothing sets out to hurt or manipulate you.

I was heading down the river for a wash. I was miles away when a whole stand of gums seemed to gallop off uphill. Because I knew there was nothing natural that made so much noise, even a big mob of roos wouldn't make so much flurry, I was at a loss as to what was happening. Perhaps it was an old mine collapsing. It sounded like a wild fire in the still heat of the day. I stood there, my mouth dry, pulse erratic, gripped by real fear. Then I realised what it was and I was scared no more. Relief swept over me. I was as relaxed as I had been before. That release is something that doesn't happen in town. It doesn't happen at home, I'm always tense. Eating, sleeping, studying— trying to study I should say. It's like there's something frightening happening every minute of the day and night. That herd of wild goats, because that was what frightened me on the way to swim, are stampeding all the time. I guess I've been that tense since the Sea Witch Stepmother moved in. Grade six was the last time I felt really relaxed. So many people must go through their whole lives in a state of fear. I won't live like that.

When I got to Ah Kow's swimming hole I floated about for ages and sunned myself naked. I'm not self-conscious at all now—it's not that I'm confident that no one is coming, although I know now I would hear anyone coming, but because I don't bloody care who sees me. I must admit I am a little proud that I've lost a couple of kilos, it's the lean diet, no butter, red meat, cheese. I'm a lot more active too, just doing the daily chores; water and wood have to be carried. It's pretty hilly round here. I must be much fitter, pretty tanned too, despite wearing the hat all the time. I need a haircut but I can't justify the money and I've only got the mini scissors on the Swiss army knife. It doesn't matter what I look like out here but I'd like some of the girls at school to see my new bod. So much for escaping the shit at school.

How long do I need to stay out here before I'm a real feral?

I guess I'd just be like the goats. The billy is a big grey beast with impressive horns. He could have been the original runaway. I suppose he could have sprung from the goats the miners brought with them. The nannies look like they could have been lured away from the hobby farms that surround the National Park. They look a different breed, Anglo-Nubian or some such—probably pure bred but hanging out with this wild man of the bush. The kids look a real mix. There are probably fifteen all up. If there was some way of taming them I wouldn't have to use up all my funds—goat's milk, cheese if I can work out how to make it, maybe even meat.

I can't imagine killing a kid. I've thought about wallaby stew if I could find a way of catching them. I'd have to be pretty hungry. I'm out of jam and I'm get-ting sick of damper every day. I saw a couple of rusty sheets of corrugated iron up near the road. I might drag them down and try to build some sort of roomier shelter, so I can cook in the rain, plus have something to keep the sun off. Each time I make myself more settled, dig a toilet, make a bracken bed, I ask myself how long do I intend to be out here? Does there come *a point where you never go back? What is the alter-native? Can I ignore the rest of the world, will there come a time when I need someone? Maybe I'll find a wild bushman, like the billygoat.*

I guess I should sort through some garbage. Like what brought me here, why are my peers still labouring through their final-year studies and I'm here watching the last light kiss the clearing goodnight, writing in my journal for no one else but me, with no thought of tomorrow? Where did I go off the rails? Am I just like Mum? Am I crazy, manic, skitzoid? I wish I knew what these words really mean, medically. Dad says Mum was manic, but does that mean manic-depression? I think it was just a breakdown from living with Dad. Why are men so selfish?

I know that manic-depression can be inherited. I wonder if I can get a book and find out. I don't feel crazy, not out here anyway. I've never felt so sane. I really felt like I was going insane, living in that house, going to that school. But maybe that is what being crazy means; doing something outrageous and feeling normal.

I'm not sure why I get so angry. I just do. Like when we're supposed to be writing a piece for English, Mrs French says write what you're thinking and feeling.

Dear Mrs French

I don't know what the hell I think. What would you know about thinking and feeling? You're a devotee of Transcendental Meditation; seems to me like meditation is anti-thought. You're content to drift along, how can you expect to teach teenagers when you escape existence every chance. Maybe I should hand this in. Then we might see how serene you are. I've seen you angry—deep down you really miss the cane. I tend to believe my older cousin; you took up meditation after you had a massive breakdown. So you can shove ya thinking and feeling up ya 'celibate by choice' arse.

I can't believe she actually told us she was 'celibate by choice'! Who could she make it with? In her case it's like saying 'ugly by choice'.

I'm not sure I think, really think. Not in that logical, clear way. Things half felt, seething uncertainty, the stuff I write just ends up being confused. They think I have a negative attitude. I think negative attitude is the one thing they can't hack. They say you can write anything, but they lie. I know one girl who wrote a love story, it just happened to be pretty sexy and she got shit. I think they objected more to how or why they did it, rather than the fact that they did it. The girl did it because she had really low self-esteem, she thought she was ugly or unlovable, so she screwed so someone would like her—definitely not politically correct. But it happens. Happens all the time. I think we're too young to be liberated.

There is no real freedom. Sex is just one of the things you can't talk about. No one really writes love stories in English. No one says you can't, everyone just knows you don't. Lots of teachers have kids, you'd think some of them would have fallen in love. Perhaps all the English teachers were too busy reading to fall in love. Is that just another sort of escape? Where is the passion?

How did I get thinking about school? I guess I was imagining what they would be doing—I must get some books. This next trip to town could be expensive. I want to know the names of these birds. I watched these rosellas this morning, except they weren't crimson ones, they were mostly green, so colourful they were garish. We think of the bush being drab! I've never seen colours so vivid, so strident.

Shopping list
Seeds for vegies
Meat
Rope
Books to read
Soap
Toothpaste

Candles, kero lamp
Flour
Food, food, food
Spade for new dunnies
Excitement, sex, drugs
Music (batteries)

I worry a lot about running out of food. I've still got plenty of money for the time being, but I'm just running it down. There won't be any more. I've been wondering if I could kill to eat. There are wallabies, goat, and even sheep in paddocks not too far away. Am I just a spoilt school kid camping out or is this for real? Could I not go back, ever? Can I survive? What price am I prepared to pay? So far I have simply run away, avoided a life, temporarily.

Can I make a new life? I remember Dad telling the Step-Serpent when Monique moved out, 'She'll be back within a week, leave her bed made up'. Monique was nineteen, had a Course, and friends to share the house. I know Dad does not understand how much we hate Medusa the Step-Mom. I have just run away, no house, no future, no final exams, no fuckin nothing, no friends, no family, thank God! What am I doing? If I went back now I could finish my finals. I'd probably get consideration of disadvantage. I wonder if they know at school.

Sometimes I think that this life here is all that there ever was. I have lost all track of time. I know that I should miss TV and stuff, but I've got music, tapes anyway. Maybe I should have a radio, but I didn't really listen to it. The world could end. I guess I'd know when the jets stopped going over.

I bought a rope. I've been trying to snare that old billy-goat for two days—I figure the others will hang around if I can catch him. I sat in the native cherry tree that the goats seem to frequent, waiting. I put a loop on the ground waiting for him to step into it. He wouldn't. One of the kids did, so I pulled the rope. The goat flipped base over and headed off into the scrub. Then I had a bright idea, that I could drop the loop over the horns. I had to wait another full day until the goats returned. I waited patiently like a native hunter. The billy walked straight up to the tree, I dropped the loop, it closed beautifully over the great curved horns. He took off, I hung onto the rope, I flew out of the tree, I hit the ground. I was embarrassed and there was no one there to see.

The bastard ran off with my rope. I have gravel rash up my front. I laughed myself sick, lying there in the dust. I laughed until I cried. It was the stupidest day. I had such a good time. I'm worried though that the rope might get snagged on something and hurt the goat. I'll have to keep hunting until I can find him. How I get the rope off I don't yet know.

I think I'm a bit of a fugitive. I noticed this hole in the stone cliff above the river. I suppose it's a cave really. I only noticed it because some birds seem to be using it and I was on the far side of the river. It is difficult to spot because there is a tree in the way. The tree grows right out of the rock. You have to actually lower your-self over the edge of the cliff until your feet go into the hole.

It's big enough to stand up in. If you go right inside it's surprisingly dry. You get a great view from the mouth of the hole. It was okay getting in but freaky get-ting out—there is nothing to grab hold of and you have to just slide your hands up the roots on the face of the rock and then lever yourself up onto the ledge. If you slip you land in a nice deep pool, that's if you don't crack your head open on the edge. It's a great place to hide, though. No one would ever find you. I might need it as a dry storehouse, if I'm here in winter.

It's time I did some clear thinking. Was life so bad? It does not matter. This is so much better. I have days I don't notice, dreary maybe, but really relaxed. I have moments where I feel absolutely one with this place. The deep green of the evening—there is this khaki light, the trees almost turn black against the pale pearl of the evening sky. My soul sings, I get this surge of well being, I lie down on the cooling earth and I know I'm home. I've lived in houses since Mum left. Mum is here. I think she'd like this. If this is crazy, then crazy I want to be.

———————

When Tommo and I were going out, I was losing my head. I remember reading this book and not being able to tell what was real. Men are such bastards but women know with confidence what they need. They are so much more in touch; that's why the Scorpion Step-Bitch is satisfied with her misery and Dad is just plain miserable. I have moments of regret. This must be cruel for him. He's spineless but he probably doesn't deserve what Madam Bile has done to him. She'll survive okay. Women deal with misery better; it's part of child-bearing, each child is like having another heart, another heart to break. Dad will look back and feel cheated, he'll realise he's been used, at least I hope he does.

I understand why Dad never learned to survive on his own. He let Mum do everything. When she lost it, spent days staring at the wall, stopped doing the housework as well as her own work, he felt lost, unable to cope. He couldn't move out of his set pattern. Instead of facing the darkness he just changed the light bulb. Sent Mum off to the loony bin. She challenged him to cope, needed him to be strong for once. He just got someone to take her place, someone who would demand nothing. Someone to take charge, spineless bastard. He forgot about us, and did she take charge! She moved in before they were officially separated. She ran the whole divorce. I still think Mum was ripped off. Mum's not concerned— says she is better off without his money. I wonder where she is now.

Not one of my friends has happy parents. Why do they do it? They stay together for the kids. Trouble is, I think they're doing their kids a disservice. Sure kids get stuffed up when parents split, but they get stuffed up living in stuffed homes, too. And they learn that life is that dreadful half-lived, nowhere land of not-so-quiet desperation.

I wrote a whole essay on quiet desperation. Mrs French said to write about what you know.

I found the goat rope. Guess I get to fall out of a tree again.

I guess I'm finally bored. It rained all day. I still went for a walk. It's raining again, although it's still warm. I wanted to write but I sat there with the pen poised and it was like a slow movie of memories. Maudlin, that's what I am maudlin, sad for no particular reason. I lay here and these pictures raced through my head; Mum red-faced behind her glasses, screaming that she wants him to leave her alone, Dad slapping her face, pretending he was trying to calm her down. I saw the lie. He was just embarrassed. He was punishing her for not being able to cope with his oppression. I will never forgive him that. Mum sitting, crying and crying, sitting in the foyer of the hospital in that blue towelling dressing-gown. It felt like I was the mother, she seemed so small. Dad's face going up the stairs of the hospital, petrified, not of what had happened to Mum but just the place, the loonies. He almost ran out afterwards. Scared of catching it, like it might stick to his clothes. If he ever tries to touch me, I'll kill him. He'll not put me away.

I didn't go back to school that day, Dad said I could go to the pool instead. No one else was there, just me in this huge pool. I felt really guilty—Mum was sick so I take the day off to celebrate. Me listless, floating around on my back and just losing interest in staying afloat, sliding under the water, wondering if drowning was like losing your mind.

Then the next day walking into school from the bus thinking that they could tell that I had been in touch with insanity.

I thought everyone knew that my mother was a loony. I was so ashamed. Now I'm really ashamed, that I felt that. It was so selfish. I used to get so angry at them, the kids, the young, they seemed so immature, so petty, I consciously isolated myself. I guess that was when I started chewing the skin on my hands and around my nails until they bled. I couldn't stop. I just realised that they are completely healed for the first time in years. They are pink with new skin, at least under the dirt they're pink.

I was thinking about the last school assembly, I remember blinking up at the faded blue of sky, the distant wisps of cloud as interested in the school assembly as I.

Quiet desperation grows out of tirades. Tirade was the only way to describe what the colourless man on the dais described as one of his little chats. It occurred to me, that if these chats were to have any effect they would have to come from someone the students respected. He was wasting his time. I guess there are a few teachers I don't hate but most I wouldn't piss on if they were on fire. I was filled with the urge to cry out and run screaming from the quadrangle—that would *really prove that I'm crazy. I took a deep breath to calm myself.*

Then as we were walking into class, Pox saw this kid heading for the door and just shouldered him into the wall, I think he was in year nine or ten. The kid scrapes himself off the wall and starts jabbing Pox in the back as they shove at the door. Pox turns around, he didn't know for sure who it was, he didn't have time to think about it, he just slammed his fist into the face of this kid. I heard a crack and Cherie screamed because she got blood on her uniform. But this kid went down and just lay there in the litter of ice-cream wrappers. Pox and his friend just laughed about it. You could tell instantly that the nose was broken. It did this right turn.

That is the atmosphere that I could have subjected myself to every day. Is the world outside school any better? Probably less physical but no less vicious. Those sorts of kids have the power. They set the tone. If you deviate from this mainstream there are punishments. There is the physical stuff but there is other stuff that is far more sinister. It is not okay to achieve. If you do, you have to pretend it was an accident. Sorry I didn't mean to write the best essay, or get the science prize, it's this genetic thing I can't help, I'd really be just as happy to fail.

Schools are so soulless. I wonder sometimes if they aren't evil. The school pretends that it serves some greater good, civilisation, or education. It's really a sausage factory. If they were really interested in learning they wouldn't get fussed about what we actually study but they make us stick to this bunch of old ideas about what is good to learn. You get excited about something, want to know, but then you have to move on.

But they've got you by the short and curlies.You need that piece of paper if you want to do anything. So you submit to this mind bending, you intern yourself in this institution of hardened haters. You end up with angry kids who don't want to learn, so the school becomes a place that is anti-learning.

For every thousand secondary school students, one will take his or her life every year. Usually it is a he. I know because I researched it in English. I wanted to do more, I wanted to know why my friends were dying but Ms Celibate-by-Choice told me I had to work on the novel. I wrote this piece after Mark hanged himself. I always thought it was 'hung', the media says hanged. He didn't hang himself though, he tied a really good knot in the ski tow-rope from the family boat and dived out of the hay shed.

When they said 'hanged' it didn't describe what he did. What he did was tear my heart out.

I don't believe he hanged himself. I believe we hanged him, his friends, his school, maybe even his family, this whole crappy world. The world was not good enough. It needed to be brighter somehow, more interesting, more beautiful.

I used to listen to the news sometimes and think of Mark. What he did made sense if our world is that depressing. I'm not saying it was the right thing, but I can understand.

I think Mark knew about quiet desperation. He had everything, but he thought he had nothing. Maybe he thought he was too tacky for this world. Maybe it needed someone braver, to take the crap, endure the drudge. Mark didn't have much endurance. Maybe he was the only brave one. He used to walk up to people and ask; 'Can you feel it?' He'd do it to little kids, teachers, strangers on the street. Then he would wait and watch, and if they asked, 'Feel what?' he'd walk away disgusted. If they just thought about it he'd just stand and wait, watching like he was searching for the reincarnation of the Dalai Lama.

I said no when he asked me. He told me to keep listening, waiting. He did this for more than twelve months. Then he stopped. Then he started drumming, da da de-dah, da da de-dah. 'It's coming!'

I wasn't very close to Mark but I did listen, did try to understand him. I thought he could hear something, knew something I didn't know. He could feel the earth pulling at him, the wind, the sound of thunder, the mind of God.

He'd make a beautiful angel. Sometimes when I sit in the stillness listening, I could swear the earth nudges me. Gives me a nudge from behind. Like the flesh of a horse it quivers and is still. So quick I doubt it.

I do remember Mark used to talk about death. He tried to explain that it was important to have it in your mind otherwise you had nothing to compare life to. All we have known is life. There must be an alternative or there is no choice. If you remember that the alternative to life is death, then when you choose to live it is a real choice. Not just living because you're too lazy to choose.

Sounds pretty confused when I read back over this. But that is what floored me when I heard that he had topped himself. He was a classic. His profile fitted all the danger signs. I didn't know there were danger signs until afterwards. They teach us all about it, afterwards.

I just thought it was Mark. He was like me, normal.

I felt really guilty, he'd shown me his thoughts; I just ignored them. Well I didn't ignore them, they just seemed like typical questions. Everyone is frustrated, it's just that most can't express themselves as well as Mark.

We were all shocked, blown away, nothing seemed to make sense. I guess that was what Mark was talking about. You can't argue with death, all our problems seemed really petty. We didn't think we were immortal any more. If Mark could die so could we. He was so full of life. He was off the wall. He shamed us with his passion, thumping on the desk after every class.

'It's coming!'

I'm not sure if 'it' was death or something else he was waiting for. Perhaps what he was waiting for never came and he realised that it probably never would. Perhaps he was waiting for answers to questions. Who am I? Where did I come from? And where the hell am I going? Maybe that's what I'm doing out here, searching for answers, finding more questions.

I wonder if he found answers at the end of that ski rope. Or did that fatal jolt snuff out the questions? I can see him sitting here beside me as I wrestle with his questions. He still has that searching for the Dalai Lama look and that knowing smile. I dreamt that he lives in the trees now. It sort of makes sense. He climbed the tree and never came down. I imagine his spirit dwelling in the trees and they have given him their patience. Strange thought that, fits though.

The thing that really upset me at the time was the way school dealt with it, or didn't. I heard about Mark at home. Dad was hovering around the phone waiting for a call when Tommo rang.

I thought at first he wanted to get back together or something, he was being that nice. It was as if he was embarrassed about what he had to say. Then he said, 'It's about Mark, he hanged himself last night.'

'What?' I asked stupidly. I'd heard. I just needed to think.

'He didn't make it home last night,' he went on. 'They went searching this morning, found him in the hay shed, stupid bastard. Must have been fooling around and done it accidentally, gotta go, see ya at school . . . ya there?'

'Yeah,' I muttered and hung up.

Dad was standing there, he knew something was up but I had to get away from him. I felt hysterical but I couldn't do it with Dad around. If he saw me like that I couldn't hate him. I realised I wanted the comfort of telling him but it would give him too much power. I would tell him but not until I had it under control. Sounds stupid, but that's the way it works.

When I rolled up to school some people hadn't heard, the rest were shocked. It was like it blew us apart. I guess we had never been too close as a year level, too many dickheads.

Instead of uniting we all seemed to split up, or ganged up with people we didn't usually hang with. It was like we were separated out by the way we dealt with the news. I still can't believe that Tanja and Nicole were actually in each other's arms.

Some kids who had been with Mark from primary school said they thought he was stupid and wrote him off. Others just thought he was selfish. Even though they had been told how deliberately he'd walked home, taken the rope from the boat and then actually leapt from the roof of the hay shed, others still denied that he'd intended to do it.

There were tears all over the place. No one turned up for class. The staff eventually herded us into the hall. They seemed really embarrassed. Tears do that, I suppose.

They did a good job really. The counsellor and a couple of others took us through a debriefing, mainly just letting people have a chance to talk about the news and their reactions. The best bit was she told us some myths about suicide, not to feel guilty, because I really did. I thought I could have stopped him if I'd taken real notice of what he was trying to say to us. Then she talked about grief and explained that what we were going through was very natural and went on to explain what we could expect as the reality sunk in.

The thing that pissed me off was the staff. They were really professional, they really looked after us but they didn't look after themselves. I thought initially that they didn't care and maybe some didn't but I could tell our old year-eight teacher who'd put a lot of time into Mark was really upset and so was one of the info-tech guys, he was pretty red-eyed. Why couldn't they share that? Too busy, too focused on getting us through. I was relieved when I saw them crying. It meant that what we were going through was okay. I was pleased—they didn't have the answers either. I only wish they had spoken to us about it. But it was taboo, something you don't talk about, like admitting the school had failed.

They were scared that if they made too big a deal about it, it would encourage others. Their fear became our fear, their silence made the grief worse. They did a great job, but after the funeral it seemed like a conspiracy of silence; we stopped talking about it too. I guess we were worried that people would think we were obsessed with suicide. I really miss Mark, I still think about what he said about death.

———

Something has been eating my pumpkin vine. I guess the goats are back.

———

The Mine!

I've moved into an old mineshaft in the side of the hill, I've got the goats, I've just had half a bottle of port. It's a party. It's been a while since I've written. I've been busy. Funny, a few days ago I didn't have enough to keep me occupied. I haven't been for a walk for days, maybe weeks, I'm having trouble keeping track of time. I'm really pleased with my new home.

I don't know about love, I don't really care about anyone, I don't miss anyone. I like my goats, the old nanny is the best. Am I a hermit? I'm feeling pretty low. I guess I'm restless. I just don't know what to do with myself. I feel like going to town. I don't need to yet. It's just I need some excitement. Some hermit!

I just stopped and listened to the quiet, it was like I could hear the peace dripping from the trees. The light was low off the river, glistening, the air liquid. All the other colours disappeared and I understood why I'm here. I wasn't so much running away from something, I was running to something. Anything had to be better then the tepid life I was living back in town. This is where I should be, funny that yesterday I was restless—how could I leave this? This feels like home now, this cave / hut is very civilised. I can cook inside and look down the gully to the creek and beyond that to the glint of the dirty Lerdy Dergy River. I've built shelves with timber from the driftwood and I've slung a cosy bed using sacking and saplings. I'm still a bit worried about winter and money. This place could be pretty miserable. That's too far ahead to worry about, I'm just going to enjoy the sunset.

The sunset made me sad, for Dad. For some reason I'm feeling sorry for him. I think it might be autumn coming on. We speak of things only if they don't matter. The conspiracy of silence. I am sorry for Dad because he has lost his daughter. I have come to the wilderness and found the wilderness in myself. I will defend it against all intruders.

My first night here was a nightmare of fear, every shadow was a threat. Now I know each shadow intimately, the shadows are now my refuge. The bush exhales, I inhale, she drips, I cry. Our silence our bond; I can no longer speak.

Now the only thing I really fear is someone walking up my gully. They would threaten my silence. My father will not pry a word from me. Whatever power he had over me has gone. The bush will sense his noisy hostility and punish him. No sound will be dragged from me. I fear the violence my words might do.

The words are the same, the meanings are unrecognisable. People never did listen anyway, all too busy thinking about what they wanted to say next. There was no silence in our lives. I think the racket of humanity would strike me deaf.

―――――――

I was on my log, sitting, staring into the fire, I'd never realised how many colours there are in fire. There is a colour the same as the back of those rosellas. A purple that dances sensuously with the green, writhes with the gold, flickers independently of the rest of the flame.

I am flame, flickering independently of the rest of the fire. Can I burn alone? How long can I burn before I run out of fuel? Do I need the rest of the human fire to survive? I just had a vision of myself, I seem to have lost a lot more weight. I am lean, a shadow, the still- ness is not disturbed by my passing. A cold blue flame, I am transparent.

I don't think this is the same brain I came out here with.

―――――――

They are searching, I heard the bus hours ago, I could hear their violence from the next valley. I loathe them, they come to violate my space, invade my sanctuary, monster my silence. I decided they should find no part of me, no trace. They would stomp around my wilderness with their high-tech gear, their radios, their fucking good intentions. A macho picnic, coming to the rescue of this poor girl lost in the bush. I am truly lost to the bush, they would never understand.

I've covered all the evidence, I have never been here. I wait, there is no need to run from them, they will never find me. They are moving very slowly. I don't think they have come to search, they are moving very slowly because one of the girls keeps collapsing, their packs are huge! It's the year-ten camp, they're not searching, just invading. I cannot believe it is the same camp I did two years ago. Either the camp is earlier this year or I've been here much longer than I thought. I actually know some of them.

The only way they could catch me is if I choose to be caught. I wonder what nonsense they will talk around the fire tonight. There used to be a part of me that would like to sit at the fire, walk back into the arms of the human race but as I watched them discreetly from the ridge above I loathed them.

I stood in the shadow of the trees and saw myself as someone else might; I've become the wild woman of the gorge. At the same time I now blend into the bush, I belong.

I have painted my face yellow ochre, I am in mourning for the silence. I have hacked all my hair off. Something inside has broken. I am shattered like a crystal. I keep crying tears of joy. It will never be rejoined. The hair will make a great pillow. I will never be the same, I will never go back. I can never go back.

Before one of them screamed I crept close enough to hear them telling stories of parties, deb balls, boyfriends and a letter about a girl. A girl who has a darkness in her. I have a black pit.

How could they have ever upset me? I have nothing in common with them. They saw me. One of them even tried to chase me.

I pitied them their need for each other, their pathetic sense that they have some mastery over the environment, crashing along in their boots. Even the games they play with each other, the dishonesty of swimsuits, the hollow bravado of the boys, the verbal shit-stirring—pathetic. But the noise! They bellow when they talk, shout and guffaw like bad-mannered pigs. They have no respect. No Respect.

There is blood on the page. I have chewed all around my fingernails again. Those bastards. They do *not belong here. They do not belong anywhere, they are an aberration. They are the viruses that threaten to destroy the planet. They threaten my peace, my space, my harmony.*

I crossed the river and listened to their stories again. They were telling the story of a girl, a girl in the bush, a girl bound by silence. This is too freaky! They can't know. They have no right to tell my story. THEY DO NOT, CAN NOT KNOW ME.

I realise now what violence would have been inflicted on the beautiful indigenous cultures of the planet as the colonial barbarians clumped their way across their piece of paradise. I just want them out of my part of the world. I want my river back, my silence. I do not want them to know I am here. I do not want them to know I exist. I hated their wars, their news, their economy, their insurance, their complexity, their technology. I have never belonged to them, I will never belong. Never.

They have made it to Ah Kow's. I can hear them from here. They pollute my home. I will move to the cave.

I can feel the pull of the sea, I'm going to the sea. I want to feel the spray and smell the seaweed. I want to lie in the surf and let the waves carry me in and out. I have prickles embedded in me, all over. I felt nothing when I ran through them a couple of nights ago. Now they feel like the group down by my river, an inflammation, an infection.

He is here. My father has come. I saw him. He didn't try to chase me, he just tried to speak to me. He is waiting. He is too late, too late, too late toolate toolate.

the last bit:
here's your epic back

I can't recall half of the things I thought while we were reading the diary or much of the conversation afterwards. There was so much about her diary that we had used in the epic. We knew who she was; she went to our school. I say we knew her but none of us were her friends. She was really quiet at school. We all knew Mark though, the guy who topped himself. We were only in year ten, so we didn't know him as well as the girl who wrote the diary. As far as we knew, this girl was no rebel, she always wore her uniform—it seems she just ran away from home and school for three months and occasionally stabbed her father!

We also knew the school, the teachers and the school environment she ran away from. We could understand her feelings about school but we ended up discussing if it was that bad.

I can't get my head straight. I kept getting confused. As we were reading the diary I kept thinking that she was the blue girl in the epic. I kept waiting for the part where she went home from the party in the blue windcheater. If I tell the truth I wanted her to meet the guy with the blue gecko on his forehead.

I can't separate the epic from the girl who wrote the diary. It makes sense in a way; what happened in the bush with Becc and the girl in the cave, Matt down the shaft. Stabbing her father was the real end of the epic. Our story and the girl's story had become one. The epic had become reality. No wonder I still get confused, that's one of the reasons I'm writing this down, I'm just trying to separate the truth from fiction. I know what really happened and what we made up, but there are so many layers and versions that my brain just lets it slip and I'm back where I started. I guess it's not all that important. Becc reckons the epic isn't over till I return the girl's diary and her knife.

I'm not sure how all these stories became my stories but, as Mungrel says, we share the epic. I'm just not too sure how much I should share. I know I shouldn't mention her name. And I feel guilty that I picked up the diary the next morning and maybe I shouldn't let anyone else see it. Mungrel wanted to know what happened in the epic while he was off helping Adam, so here it is. I also feel it is like in the epic, her story needs to be told or you disturb the order—some guy with a blue gecko on his forehead will come looking for me. It's not a happy story but it should be told. I think, sometimes, maybe the girl would want me to tell her story.

That day we limped our way out of the gorge, we didn't talk much; we just walked along with our own epics in our heads. This is just my version. The girl's father talked about searching for his daughter. He was determined to go back and find her. I wonder if he ever will. I felt really sorry for him and wondered if his daughter was really happy out in the gorge. I should return her diary and her knife; maybe I will.

It's Becc's obsession to go back to try and help the girl but I keep telling her if she stabs her own father she will not listen to us. I think I might like to take the girl my version of the epic, though. I have this vision of taking the epic to the blue girl who we thought was the yella fella.

I think about her a lot. Her diary just tries to answer the scariest question, 'What does it all mean?' She's got me doing it now. I guess that is why I've done no homework for weeks and written all this down. I'm just trying to make sense of it all.

Maybe that is what telling stories is all about, eh, Mr Mungrel? Just trying to make sense of it all? Anyway here is your epic back.

As I sit here I feel a bit depressed. The writing is over; I'm going to miss it. I understand now that the story is more real than the writing. The writing is over for now, but the story ... I don't seem to have much control over the story.